# Esme Higgs
## and Jo Cotterill

# Ellie and the Pony Camp Mystery

Illustrated by Hannah George

**PUFFIN**

PUFFIN BOOKS

UK | USA | Canada | Ireland | Australia
India | New Zealand | South Africa

Puffin Books is part of the Penguin Random House group of companies
whose addresses can be found at global.penguinrandomhouse.com

www.penguin.co.uk
www.puffin.co.uk
www.ladybird.co.uk

First published 2024

001

Set in 10.5/20pt Merriweather
Typeset by Jouve (UK), Milton Keynes
Printed and bound in Great Britain by Clays Ltd, Elcograf S.p.A.

The authorized representative in the EEA is Penguin Random House Ireland,
Morrison Chambers, 32 Nassau Street, Dublin D02 YH68

A CIP catalogue record for this book is available from the British Library

ISBN: 978-0-241-59775-0

All correspondence to:
Puffin Books
Penguin Random House Children's
One Embassy Gardens, 8 Viaduct Gardens, London SW11 7BW

**@starlightstablesyouth** Hello, Starlight fans! Ellie here, with another post about why I LOVE riding. Lots of you already know that I use a wheelchair because I hurt my back in an accident, so riding a horse is like getting the use of my legs back. But even BEFORE the accident I was obsessed with riding! There's something so magical about being on a pony, isn't there? Horses are such amazing creatures, so clever and loving. At Starlight Stables, I usually ride a beautiful Connemara called Carmen, but today I'm trying out a new pony and I can't WAIT! Hit that follow button to find out how I get on – and stay tuned for more Starlight news from me and my fellow Youth Ambassadors: Daniel, Summer and Jessie! Mwah! Ellie xx

#horsesaremylife #ilovehorses
#ponymad #starlightstablesgang #ssg

# Chapter 1

I don't know if *you* have something that makes you happy, calm; something you live for, something that makes the week easier to get through ... well, for me, that's riding. Just getting ready for my lesson every Saturday, pulling on jodhpurs and boots, getting in the car, driving to Starlight Stables ... my tummy flip-flops all over the place as Dad pulls up in the car park. Today, Mum's with us because I'm trying out a new pony, but before my lesson I'm desperate to catch up with my gang friends.

Jessie and Summer are already in the yard when I zoom in – and I can see Daniel's mop of brown hair sticking over the top of one of the stable doors as he mucks it out. My tummy flip-flops have *nothing* to do with Daniel; I just want to make that *quite clear*.

'Gang!' I yell, and everyone grins at me.

'Is it the afternoon already?' says Daniel, looking surprised.

'Did you forget to eat lunch?' I ask.

He makes a silly face. 'I didn't forget to eat it; I forgot to pack any.'

Daniel's mum works two jobs and he has FIVE younger siblings, so their house is a bit chaotic. Daniel basically looks after his younger brothers and sisters, even though he's only thirteen.

'*Daniel!*' says Summer, looking scandalized (which is one of my favourite words). 'Have one of my sandwiches – I didn't finish them today.'

'I've got some crisps you can have,' offers Jessie.

Daniel turns pink and mumbles, 'Thanks, I'll just finish this job first.' He starts shovelling the shavings with renewed energy.

'Is it today you're trying the new pony?' Summer asks me. She's wearing a new riding top that I know she bought with money she made selling drawings. Summer is a brilliant artist.

I nod. 'I am *so* excited. Alice thinks he'll suit me better than Carmen. She says he's been amazing in her other lessons.'

'How exciting,' says Jessie, but then I see her face fall. Jessie fell off her pony Angus a while back and got concussion and even though she's allowed to ride now, she gets really anxious on horseback. It's a shame because Jessie is an amazing rider and showjumper.

'Did you have a lesson today?' I ask hesitantly.

She shakes her head and her long plait flips over one shoulder. 'Maybe in another couple of weeks.'

'You'll get there,' I say with certainty.

'*I* did a trot with a changing rein,' Summer tells me proudly. 'In a figure of eight.'

'Hey, that's brilliant!' I high-five her.

'I did it in a canter,' Daniel calls.

'You never!'

'Did too.'

Summer and Daniel have only been riding a few weeks, but Daniel's already amazing at it. I think Summer is a bit envious.

'We might not still be here at the end of your lesson,' Summer tells me. 'Message the group chat to let us know how it goes!'

'Or tell us next week,' says Jessie with a smile. 'At school.'

'Yay!' I beam back at her. 'Can't believe we're all going to be in the same school. The Starlight Stables Gang together!'

'Hey,' says Daniel. 'Not *all* the gang.'

'Sorry, Daniel,' I say. 'You need to transfer to ours!'

'Ellie!' I turn to see Jodie heading into the courtyard. She and Sooz own and run Starlight Stables. Today, she's wearing a navy T-shirt with the Starlight logo and a pair of jeans tucked into wellies. 'Great to see you. I want to talk to you about

6

advertising some half-term pony days on social media.'

'Sure,' I say. I basically run the Starlight Stables social media accounts. I love making reels and writing posts and we're gaining followers at a gallop! 'Ooh, pony days – can I come?'

She grins at me. 'If you get your parents to book, yes.'

'No,' Jessie says suddenly. 'No, don't go in half-term: I heard that Berry Farm is doing a pony camp then.'

Summer, Daniel and I immediately swing round to her. 'A pony camp?'

'Is it as good as everyone says?' I ask.

'Better.' Jessie's eyes shine. 'You get to ride every day, there are barbecues and games and midnight feasts, and everything.'

'Ohmygosh,' says Summer. 'That sounds amazing.'

'Are you going to spend the half-term at our biggest rival?' Jodie says, her eyes twinkling. 'Our Youth Ambassadors, abandoning Starlight Stables for Berry Farm? I'm *outraged*.' She doesn't sound outraged, mind you.

'You could run a pony camp here,' suggests Summer.

Jodie laughs. 'I would love to, but we don't have the facilities. It's all right, you go off to Berry Farm. It's a great opportunity! Ellie, I'll send you an email with all the information for the pony days.'

'OK.' I nod.

As Jodie disappears, Summer says in a low voice, 'What does pony camp cost, Jessie? You know I don't have much money.'

'Me neither,' says Daniel cheerfully. 'Not a penny.'

'Oh.' Jessie looks disconcerted. 'I don't know. Maybe the charity that runs your lessons could help?'

'Speaking of charity lessons,' I say, glancing at my phone, 'it's time for mine! See you in a bit!'

I wheel round to the indoor school, where my parents are chatting to my Riding for the Disabled instructor, Alice. Alice is holding a pony I don't recognize, and my heart quickens. This must be the new pony I'm trying out!

'Ellie.' Alice smiles at me. 'Say hello to Elvis.'

Elvis is a piebald cob with feathery feet and a budding moustache. He's definitely not a film-star pony like an Akhal-Teke! But as I head over, he turns to look at me, and my tummy melts, like it always does whenever I see a horse. 'Hi, Elvis,' I say, and he bends down so I can stroke his nose. His mane is half-white, half-black, like Cruella de Vil.

'Elvis has had a lot of experience of riders who give verbal instructions, and he's super-sensitive,' Alice tells me. 'I think he's going to be perfect for you, Ellie. Let's get you on board.'

Starlight Stables has a hoist at the edge of the indoor ring. It's not something people generally notice but it's vital for me because I can't get myself up on to a horse. It's like a kind of sling chair – I slide into it, and it lifts me up and over the horse.

Elvis is rock-steady as I land in the saddle, unlike Carmen who sometimes wriggles a bit. 'Hello, boy,' I say softly, reaching forward to pat his neck. I settle the reins in my hands and wait for Alice to walk round and put my feet in the stirrups. I have what's called a complete spinal cord injury, which means I have no control over anything below a certain point in my back, so I can't move my own legs or feet. Alice secures my boots to the stirrups with rubber bands so that they don't slip out while I ride. Elvis stays completely still, not even shifting his weight.

'Right,' says Alice, checking that everything is secure and handing me my two whips, 'let's start with a nice slow walk around the school.'

I'm lucky to have lessons by myself. Most people learn to ride in groups but because no one else at Starlight has my specific disability, my parents asked if I could have individual lessons. Before my accident two years ago (I fell off a wall), I had weekly riding lessons, and I was desperate to get back in the saddle. When everything changes, you really want to hold on to the things you love. And don't think Alice goes easy on me because I can't walk! She's quite a tough teacher, but I like that.

'Come on then, Elvis,' I say. I touch him lightly with the whips and he moves forward in a nice, slow gait. Because I can't squeeze with my legs, I use the whips to send messages to Elvis instead by touching him lightly on his sides. Some people don't like the idea of using a whip, and I would never use one to hit a horse, but they're essential in helping me communicate with my pony.

Getting to know a new horse is a bit like meeting a new person. You don't know if you're going to 'click' with them, or whether you'll misunderstand each other. Within two minutes, I can tell that Elvis is special. He responds instantly to the slightest pressure on the reins and turns obediently in the direction I want him to go. We try circles and figures of eight and diagonals, and he's sooooo easy to ride!

'Wow,' I say, when I bring him to a halt. 'I never realized how tricky Carmen was before!'

Alice laughs. 'She's a good pony, but Elvis definitely has a better temperament. He's very empathetic.'

'I love him,' I say, giving him a pat. 'Can I trot?'

'Yes, I don't see why not.' Alice glances over to my parents, who are standing at the open end of the

school, watching. 'Don't freak your parents out, though, OK?'

'Awww,' I say, feeling mischievous. 'Are you *sure*?'

Elvis trots *beautifully*. It's a little longer than Carmen's skippy trot, which actually suits me better since I don't bounce up and down so fast. He's so intuitive too – I'm literally about to start to turn him when he anticipates my movement. A feeling of pure exhilaration shoots through me. I spend so much of my time *explaining* things to people:

answering questions about how I hurt my back, what kind of help I need getting up and down things, how I go to the toilet (seriously? Mind your own business!) that this is quite a new feeling, the feeling that I don't need to explain *anything*. Elvis just knows. It's so rare that someone instinctively understands me and doesn't need me to do anything special or be anyone different from who I am.

I can imagine that other people might feel a bit tearful in my position, but I'm not the teary type. I just feel ENORMOUS ON THE INSIDE, like a helium balloon swelling and swelling, and I can't stop SMILING so much that I think my face might break. And that would STILL feel amazing!

Alice is calling to me that our time is up, but I don't want to get off Elvis, and I give him just a *little* tickle with the whip and whisper, 'Want to go a bit faster?' and again, he *knows* – and increases his speed, and now we're *flying* round the school in a canter and I shout 'Woohoo!' and Elvis's ears twitch and I know he loves it too!

Of course, my parents start in alarm, and I can see

their postures change out of the corner of my eye. Mum is gripping the fence with white knuckles, and Dad is shouting to me. I don't want to frighten them too much, so reluctantly, I bring Elvis back to a trot and then to a walk, and then I take him over to Alice, who is trying not to smile.

'That was very naughty of you,' she says in a low voice, as my parents come rushing over.

'Sorry,' I say, not at all sorry and she knows it.

'Ellie!' My mum is clutching her chest. 'You nearly gave me a heart attack! Don't *do* that!'

Dad is checking my legs and my feet, making sure nothing has got twisted or come undone. 'I don't like the way the horse took off like that,' he grumbles to Alice. 'He doesn't look as safe as you said.'

I roll my eyes. '*Dad*. It was me, I told him to go faster.'

'I promise you,' Alice says to my dad, 'Elvis is one of the safest ponies I've ever worked with. He wouldn't do anything to put Ellie in danger.' She smiles at me. 'He knows Ellie is a very capable rider.'

'Humph.' Dad still looks glower-y.

'Well, I think he's perfect,' I say, leaning forward to hug Elvis. His mane tickles my nose.

'Good,' says Alice. 'I think so too. He'll help you progress.'

Getting back into my chair after being on a horse is always disappointing: I've been so high up, and now I'm shorter than everyone else again! But then I spot Summer and Daniel coming round the corner with a wheelbarrow of mucked-out shavings. 'Mum, we don't have to rush off, do we?' I say. 'I want to help out.'

I'm not sure Mum even hears me because she's deep in conversation with Dad and Alice, so I take that as an agreement and head over to my friends. I'm brimming with excitement over riding Elvis, and because my friends are horse-mad too, they don't mind me going on and on about him as they reach the compost heap, tip out the barrow and head back to the yard for more.

Eventually, Daniel says, 'So is Elvis your boyfriend now?' and I don't know why but that makes me laugh like an idiot.

# Chapter 2

'Ellie! Time to go!'

I hit 'post' on my phone screen and tuck it into the front pocket of my bag – my brand-new school bag. Today is my first day at secondary school, AAAHHHH! I'm kind of nervous and excited at the same time. Nervosited. There, you can have that word for free. I love words. I collect them. I read loads of books, especially mystery stories, and I like using long words, even though it sometimes confuses my friends.

'Ellie.' My dad comes into my bedroom, looking tetchy ('tetchy' is a word I picked up from my nan. You can probably guess what it means). 'Didn't you hear me? It's time to go.'

'All right, all right.' I pick up my school bag and dump it on my legs, then wheel myself out of my room, into the hall and out of the front door to the car. When I had my accident, Mum and Dad had an extension built on to the side of the house so I could have a downstairs bedroom and bathroom. Their bedroom is still upstairs, but I have a kind of intercom system so I can call them if I need help.

I transfer into the car and Dad packs my wheelchair into the boot. Mum comes running out of the house, still trying to put on her lipstick. 'My *darling*,' she says, leaning over to kiss me.

I pull back. 'Nooooo! Don't make me all pinkystick!'

She fusses me, putting my seat belt on even though I can do it perfectly well myself. 'Have you

17

got your packed lunch? Water bottle? Laptop? Money for snacks?'

'Muuuuum,' I moan.

Dad gets into the car and starts the engine, pointedly. Mum dithers on the driveway. 'I should come with you,' she says.

'*No*,' I say firmly. Then I feel bad because she looks kind of sad and worried, so I say more kindly, 'I'll be fine, Mum. It's me, remember?'

'Go on, then.' She wipes an eye. 'Go and be brilliant.'

Dad pulls away and I wave at Mum until we're out of sight. Then I check my hair in my phone camera. Today my Afro is pulled back into two bunches, each secured with a black hairband. My school doesn't allow dyed hair, or nail varnish, or fancy jewellery – all the things I like! Normally, I have bright beads or pink tips or coloured threads running through my hair, but not today. The uniform is very dark – black trousers, a grey jumper with a black stripe, black shoes. It makes me feel not very like *me*, which makes me nervous.

But as soon as we pull up in the school car park, I see Jessie and Summer waving, and instantly I feel MILES better! 'Hey!' I say, beaming as I get back into my chair and wheel towards them. 'Aren't you here way too early?'

Summer smiles at me. 'We couldn't let you go in alone, not on the first day.'

'We wanted to get here early to surprise you,' adds Jessie. 'Wow, your hair looks so ... ordinary.'

'I know, right?' I pat the bunches, scowling. 'I hate it.'

Dad hovers. 'Should I come in with you?'

'No,' I say. 'I know where to go.'

'We'll take her to her form room,' Jessie tells him. 'Don't worry.'

Other kids are arriving, walking up the driveway and staring at my chair. I'm kind of used to it – everybody stares – but I don't want them thinking I need my dad for everything. 'See you later, Dad!' I call, and the three of us set off, round the side of the main building into one of the two playgrounds.

'I was so nervous when I came,' Summer tells me. 'At least you're starting at the beginning of the year. Everyone in your form is new, so they'll all be nervous.'

Summer joined this school late last year when her parents split up and she had to move. She and Jessie are in the year above me, so they already know their way around. I like meeting new people, but I'm really glad they'll be looking out for me here!

The school arranged for my form teacher, Mr Claremont, to meet me in the form room early, along with Miss Mathyruban, who's a teaching assistant. But when we get there, the form room is empty.

'Huh,' says Jessie, looking around. 'They definitely said to meet here, yeah?'

'Yes,' I say. 'Miss Mathyruban is going to come with me all day today, making sure I can get to my classes.'

'The corridors get mega crowded in between lessons.' Summer looks worried. 'I hope you won't get squashed.'

'I get to leave early,' I tell her, grinning. 'To avoid the rush!'

Another student comes into the room. He's tall, with dark skin and black hair like me, and his eyes go straight to me and my chair, even though Summer and Jessie are here too. 'Oh,' he says. 'Are you in this form too?'

'Yep,' I say cheerfully. 'I'm Ellie, hi.'

'Oh,' he says again. 'Right.' A slight crease appears between his eyebrows, like someone has pinched the skin. Then he turns and walks straight out of the room.

There is a slightly awkward pause. 'Wow,' says Jessie. '*Rude*.'

'I'm sure he didn't mean to be,' says Summer uncertainly. Summer is the kind of person who wants to think the best of everyone.

I'm a very confident person, but sometimes even I can feel a bit wobbly. Being disabled often means that people are rude to you accidentally – and sometimes on purpose. But I'm determined not to let anyone see me upset or worried. That's not how you make friends. And it's important that I make friends in my form.

Before any of us can say anything else, however, Mr Claremont comes into the room at top speed. He's kind of posh-looking, with floppy blond hair and geeky glasses. 'Ellie!' he exclaims. 'So sorry I'm late. Where's Miss Mathyruban?' He looks around the room as if expecting her to pop up from behind a table or out of a cupboard.

'Not here yet,' I tell him.

'Right, right, well, never mind. You've got your timetable, haven't you? And —' he blinks for a moment, suddenly noticing Jessie and Summer — 'ah, you have some — friends with you? Are you in my form?'

'Oh, no,' says Jessie. 'We're in Year Eight. Ellie's our friend; we're just keeping her company.'

'Excellent, excellent.' Mr Claremont glances at the clock. 'Well, you'd better be getting along yourselves. Ellie, we're starting with an assembly in the hall for all the new Year Sevens. I'll take you along — and we can track down Miss Mathyruban on the way, I hope.' He bustles to his desk and picks up a binder.

Jessie and Summer look at me. 'You'll be OK?' asks Summer – a question not a statement.

'Course,' I tell her, sounding one hundred per cent confident even though on the inside I'm maybe only seventy-three per cent OK. 'See you at break?'

'We'll find you,' Jessie says, and even though I know that's a kind of normal friend thing to say, I also know that anyone in this school, at any time, could find me, because I am the only wheelchair user in a school of nine hundred students, and as such, I'm going to stick out like the biggest, sorest, reddest thumb ever.

My friends wave goodbye and vanish, and Mr Claremont says, 'Right then, off we go,' and suddenly we're heading down the corridor towards a hall full of students, and every single one of them will notice me, guaranteed.

Weds 6ᵗʰ September

Hooooooome! What a day. What. A. Day. I'm glad it's over, TBH. Tomorrow will be easier, I think. Most people were nice - only four people asked me, 'What happened to you/ why are you in a wheelchair?' which I count as a WIN.

Miss Mathyruban is a bit ... flaky? I met her last term when I went in for my transition days, but back then she seemed really nice and on top of things, and today she was all flustered. I kept having to remind her that we had to leave a bit early for each lesson, and I don't think she properly planned out my route, because when we went from maths to history, she took me down a corridor that had four steps and no ramp or lift. She went all red and asked if she could lift me down the steps because the bell was about to go, and I said no, and then it was like she didn't know what to do. So we stayed in the corridor while she tried to decide which route to take instead, and THEN the bell went and everyone came out and I was practically crushed! Miss M took hold of my handles even though she knows she's supposed to ask first, and steered me outside, and then we found another way round.

APART from that, the lessons were really fun! And the people in my form are mostly nice, especially a girl called Molly who's quite shy but who asked me about my brand-new Case Notes book. I got it because I read LOADS of mystery stories, and the detective always writes everything down in a notebook. I told Molly about the Mystery of the Missing Pony, when Luna got stolen from Starlight in the summer, and I helped find her again. From now on, I'm going to write down anything that seems odd or mysterious in my Case Notes book – that way I'll be prepared if something like that happens again. Molly was very impressed. I told her I'm going to be a detective when I'm older. Well, a detective OR an equestrian OR a film-maker – I haven't decided yet.

Jessie and Summer came to find me at break and lunch and I introduced them to Molly, but she got shy and ran away. Molly is a bit of a mystery, TBH. But not the sort you write Case Notes about.

Dad says I have to go to sleep now, Diary, so SEE YA, WOULDN'T WANNA BE YA!

# Chapter 3

At the end of my first week in school, I feel really tired. Just getting around is so exhausting, and being the only wheelchair user means I get stared at wherever I go. I'm hoping after a while people will stop doing that ... This morning, I'm yawning so much that Mum suggests I skip my riding lesson. AS IF!!! No way am I missing my favourite part of the week! It's my second lesson on Elvis and he's

PERFECT again. When we've finished, I go to find my friends. I'm dying to ask Jessie more about pony camp. We keep discussing it in the group chat, but I haven't yet talked to my parents about it. The more I think about it, the more I'm desperate to go.

Saturday is always the busiest day at Starlight. A couple of boys are leading ponies to the outdoor arena, while a girl wearing a brand-new outfit in light blue, complete with matching hat silk, is beaming as she mounts Jasper, a little chestnut cob. Sooz, one of Starlight's co-owners, is chatting cheerfully to her. Starlight houses thirty horses and ponies, a handful of which are privately owned, like Jessie's pony Angus. At any one time, up to ten horses could be tacked up and in lessons or out on woodland walks, which can be booked for parties. So the yard does get pretty busy!

Summer, Daniel and Jessie are doing stable chores at the far end. As I steer round the cracks in the ground, the people and the ponies, I can see Jessie standing next to Nacho, the chestnut cob with the white blaze, like a thick white stripe down his nose. He's contentedly chomping on a hay net, but Jessie is looking around like she's forgotten something. 'What's up?' I ask.

'Can you see the pink dandy brush anywhere?' Jessie asks, sounding puzzled. 'I swear I put it down right *here*, only like two minutes ago – and now it's gone!'

I glance over the area. 'The bright pink one? No.'

'Someone else must've taken it,' says Daniel, passing with his arms full of head collars.

Jessie shakes her head. 'They couldn't have. No one else is grooming. I was just doing Nacho, and I put it down to get the hoof pick – and now . . .' She trails off. 'It was literally right here!'

'Aha!' I say, reaching behind to whip out my Case Notes book from my bag. 'This sounds like a mystery!'

'What's that?'

'My Case Notes book.'

She rolls her eyes, amused. 'You're obsessed.'

'You say "obsessed", I say "doing my job",' I tell her, clicking the end of my pen. 'Tell me everything, from the moment you had the brush in your hand to the moment you discovered it missing.'

Jessie laughs. 'All right, Sherlock Ellie.'

---

Case #14: The Missing Dandy Brush

Location: Starlight Stables, yard

Date: Saturday 9th September

Time: 3.06 p.m.

Witness Statement from Jessie Schüster


'I was standing here by the third stable from the right-hand corner. I tied up Nacho to the ring and fetched the pink dandy brush from the brush box which was over by Angus's stable. I groomed Nacho thoroughly and then I put down the brush on the ground by the stable door. I went back to the brush box to collect a hoof pick and picked out three of Nacho's hooves. Then I noticed that the brush was missing. I did not see anyone near Nacho or the stable at any time.'

Suspects: There were lots of other people in the yard. Any one of them could have run over and taken the brush.

Opportunity: Jessie's back was turned for approx. two minutes while she was fetching the pick and working on Nacho's hooves. People were coming and going all the time. Would Jessie have noticed someone dashing over, grabbing the brush, and then running off?

Motives:

- Needed a brush to groom their own pony (but why not just ask?)
- Wanted to annoy Jessie (who? And why?)
- Kleptomania (this is when stealing things is a compulsion or habit)
- Wanted a keepsake (from Starlight Stables? Or something that Jessie had touched? Does Jessie have a secret admirer??)
- Some other reason

Conclusion:

I come to a halt, my pen suspended.

'Well?' asks Jessie.

'Hmm,' I say, playing for time. My gaze travels across the yard, over Summer coming towards us, carrying a saddle and pad. Over to Sooz, leading the little girl out of the yard. Over to the parents and kids, and the horses tied up to the rings outside the stalls. I frown. The *horses* . . .

'Look, it's fine,' Jessie says, interrupting my thoughts. 'I'll just go and get a different brush. Don't worry.'

'Stop!' I cry dramatically, lifting my pen in the air like I'm answering a question in class. 'I think I've got it!'

'What?' Jessie looks perplexed.

I turn to Nacho and brandish my pen at him dramatically. 'It was *you*, wasn't it?'

Nacho stares placidly back, his long black eyelashes fluttering slightly.

'Nacho?' repeated Jessie, baffled.

I pull open the stable door, manoeuvring my chair into the gap. 'AHA!'

On the ground, just the other side of the door, is the pink dandy brush.

Jessie gasps. 'Oh my – *what?* How did it get there?!' She comes past me to pick up the brush and stares at me in astonishment.

'Oh, you found it!' says Summer as she comes up with Nacho's saddle and bridle.

'How did you know?' demands Jessie.

I LOVE explaining how I figured something out. I put my Case Notes book and pen on my lap and clear my throat. 'Firstly, no one else was seen in the vicinity of the brush.'

'In the what?' asks Summer.

'Vicinity. Like – area. Anyone else could have come running over while Jessie was looking the other way, but people generally have excellent peripheral vision and I think Jessie would have noticed movement out of the corner of her eye –'

Summer groans. 'Would you stop with the long words!'

'If,' I continue, 'no other human was close enough to pick up the brush, then what about the very

33

obvious *non*-human right here?' We all look at Nacho, who is innocently staring at the wall. 'Nacho is intelligent and mischievous. He likes to chew your hair and nudge at your bag because he's nosy. And he has very rubbery lips. Jodie told me he once managed to unlatch a stable door when her back was turned. It would be easy peasy lemon squeezy for him to bend down, pick up the brush with his lips and toss it over the door. The work of a moment. And, of course, *a master criminal.*'

The master criminal blinks slowly.

'See!' I cry. 'He admits it! The game's up, Nacho!'

Summer and Jessie burst out laughing. 'You're so silly, Ellie,' says Jessie. 'You make him sound like James Bond or something.'

'Well,' says Summer, heaving the saddle pad and saddle on to his back, 'I think you're a genius, Ellie.'

'No, no,' I say, flapping my hand modestly. 'It's simply deduction. *When you have eliminated all which is impossible, then whatever remains, however improbable, must be the truth.* Sherlock Holmes said that.'

'Girls!' Jodie comes striding towards us. 'Is Nacho ready? We need him in the outdoor school.'

'Oh, sorry.' Summer hastily finishes doing up the girth, while Jodie takes the bridle and slips it over Nacho's ears.

'Jessie,' I begin, 'have you booked on to pony camp yet?'

'I think I'm going to next week,' says Jessie. 'I loved it so much last time. Maybe it'll help me get my confidence back.'

'Sorry, girls, can you stuff some hay nets if you've got a minute?' Jodie interrupts. 'And the Top and Middle fields need poo-picking.' She leads Nacho away.

'I can poo-pick the Top Fields,' says Summer immediately, and I know why: Luna lives in Top Field Two. When Luna was stolen, Summer was REALLY upset. She and Luna have a special bond. We only just found Luna in time – the vet said she was very ill when we rescued her. She's all better now, though, and back in the field with her pony bestie Jasper.

'I can't do fields,' I say. 'But I can stuff nets.'

'I'll come with you,' offers Daniel, coming towards us with an empty wheelbarrow. 'I can pick up some fresh shavings while I'm there.'

Jessie and Summer exchange a look, and then Jessie says deliberately, 'I'll come with *you*, Summer.' They both giggle and glance at me.

'Go on then,' I say, feeling my face heat up. I don't know why, but Jessie and Summer have started to get very silly about me and Daniel. Not that there *is* a me and Daniel. *Obviously*!

Thankfully, Daniel doesn't seem to notice. He grabs the blue handles of the wheelbarrow and sets off around the side of the school to the compost heap. Anyone who knows anything about horses knows that they poo up to ten times a day!

I head to the hay store and he joins me a moment later. One of the nice things about Daniel is that he doesn't feel the need to talk all the time. Summer, Jessie and I babble on and on about all kinds of things, but Daniel is kind of quiet and I like that about him.

We start to stuff the hay nets in companionable

silence and then all of a sudden, he says: 'Ellie, can I ask you something?'

And my stomach does a kind of flip and I think maybe the tuna sandwich I had at lunchtime must have been a bit off because I feel sick. But I say, 'Yeah, sure.'

'It's Alfie,' says Daniel, frowning as he rips open a new bale of hay.

'Uh . . .'

'One of my brothers. He's ten. He's only been back at school four days but he's already in trouble. He got in with some new boys over the summer and now –' Daniel shakes his head, his lips pressing together tightly for a moment – 'now he won't listen to me, keeps talking back. Won't tidy up after himself, shouts at everyone.'

'Wow,' I say, feeling a bit out of my depth. 'Um, well, I don't know how much help I can be. I don't have any brothers.'

'No, but – do you think I should get tougher on him? Should I stop him seeing his friends?'

'What does your mum say?' I ask, trying and failing not to drop wispy bits of hay into the creases of my wheelchair.

'She's hardly ever there,' says Daniel sadly, and I feel sorry for him. Daniel's dad is in prison, so his mum works all the time to pay the bills. Daniel has to make sure his sister and four brothers get to school on time and that kind of thing. 'But even when she *is* there, she can't deal with him either. He won't listen to any of us, and he has started saying school is stupid and he might as well not bother.'

'What, you mean – not go? That sounds . . . well, I mean, no wonder you're worried.'

He looks at me for a moment. Daniel has these pale blue eyes that are almost grey but have a darker rim to the irises. All his brothers and sisters have the same colour eyes; it's quite striking. 'I am worried. I don't want him to end up . . .' He doesn't finish, but I know what he wants to say. Daniel doesn't want Alfie to end up in prison like his dad.

'He won't,' I say. 'Not while he's got you looking out for him.'

'Thing is, I get where he's coming from, you know? When Dad went away, I was angry all the time. Coming here is what saved me.' Daniel dumps a full hay net into a grey-handled barrow and starts on another. 'I'm never going to be any good at school, but that doesn't matter. I do my best there because coming here makes me feel calmer.'

'Maybe Alfie should come and work here too,' I say slowly, wondering if I'm making the worst suggestion in the world.

But Daniel's expression changes: his eyebrows rise into his hairline and his posture straightens. 'That's ... not a bad idea, Ellie. It would mean I could keep an eye on him.'

'You'd have to ask Jodie and Sooz,' I say, thinking that they probably wouldn't be thrilled to have an angry, rude ten-year-old on the yard.

'Yeah, of course,' he says. 'They've been so good to me; I wouldn't want to annoy them. But ... you know, it could be the best thing for him. Thank you.' He gives me a real, proper smile – something we don't often see from Daniel because he's quite serious usually.

My tuna sandwich gives a lurch again and I gulp. 'No problem.'

'No, seriously, thanks. Talking to you has really helped.'

My face feels very hot. 'You need a holiday,' I say, in an attempt to be light-hearted.

He laughs. 'Yeah, right.'

'I mean it! You should totally come to pony camp. A whole week with horses and the gang!'

He pauses, net in one hand, hay in the other. 'I'd love to,' he says wistfully. 'But I just don't see it happening, you know? There's too much in the way.' He grins at me. 'You'll just have to send me loads of photos when you go.'

I smile back, but inside I'm really disappointed. It won't be the same without Daniel!

Mon 11th September

Today, TWO really annoying things happened at school.

Annoying Thing 1

P.E. I had my first P.E. lesson today. Well, actually, I DIDN'T because they hadn't worked out how to include me. I was on my way to get changed with everyone else when the P.E. teacher, Mrs Hyams, stopped me in the corridor. She said she was sorry but the girls were going out to play football, and I said Yes, and? And she looked embarrassed and said I would have to watch. I didn't know what to say because I was totally confused. Why couldn't I play football? I mean yeah, I know I can't run around like everyone else, but seriously, there are wheelchair football teams and a league and everything. And they were on the AstroTurf, not the grass, so the chair would have been fine.

Anyway, she mumbled something about safety and policies and stuff and everyone who went past stared at us, and in the end I just went fine, fine, whatever because I wanted her to stop talking.

I went out to the AstroTurf and sat and watched everyone else play football. I didn't get to do anything. Nothing. Zip. ZERO.

It SUCKED.

Annoying Thing 2

I had my first art lesson today too and I was really looking forward to it, but the art block is up some steps and they'd put in a lift thing WHICH DIDN'T WORK. You have to use a special key which Miss Mathyruban didn't have, so she had to go and ask at the office. I was left sitting by the steps like an absolute LEMON while people went past and stared at me, and one or two asked if I needed any help and I was like, NO THANK YOU I'M FINE, but obvs I wasn't. And when Miss M came back with the key it made a kind of CLUNK and nothing happened. I never got to art, and when my class came out they were all like, 'Oh, Ellie, where were you??' And I was like, 'SITTING IN THE CORRIDOR WAITING FOR THE WORLD TO BE BETTER.' Well, that's what I wanted to say, but instead I smiled and pretended I didn't mind that I'd missed out.

One other thing happened that was sucky for Molly, not me. We were lining up outside the maths room when two of the boys started shouting at each other, and then a bunch more joined in. I put my hands over my ears, and eventually a teacher came and sorted it out, and our class went into the room. But Molly couldn't move. She was trembling and breathing really fast.

I didn't know much about anxiety until Jessie started having attacks after her accident. But now I know lots because she's told us what it feels like. So I stayed in the corridor with Molly and I talked to her calmly and said she would be all right in a minute. Then I got her to look at the display board outside the classroom and count the number of red things on it, because Jessie says counting things helps her sometimes. So Molly did that and she started to calm down.

The teacher came out to see what was going on, and I explained, and he asked Molly how she was and she said she was doing better. So we went in together, and Molly said thank you to me. She said she was glad I was there because not many people understood what it's like to have a panic attack.

I told Molly that not many people understood what it was like to have my kind of disability either, and we agreed that people aren't always very kind or willing to learn. And then the maths teacher said we should probably stop talking now and do some learning ourselves, so we did. And Molly gave me a totally illegal sweet under the table, so we're definitely friends now.

Ooh, text from Jessie!

# Chapter 4

**Jessie**
Hey everyone, I've finally booked for the Berry Farm pony camp! PLEASE say you're all coming too! Click on THIS LINK!

'Mum, Mum, look at this!' I wheel into the lounge where Mum is looking at a script and mouthing words into the air. She's in a drama group and they're going to put on a pantomime of *Aladdin* at Christmas. Mum's been cast as Princess Jasmine and she's really excited. She takes her acting very seriously.

I hold out my phone and Mum squints at it. 'Not so close to my face, Ellie – what is it?'

'Pony camp at Berry Farm! In the half-term. Remember I mentioned it the other day? Jessie's booked. Can I go, can I go? *Please*!'

Mum looks taken aback. 'Is it being run by Riding for the Disabled? I didn't know they did camps.'

'No, it's just the people at Berry Farm. You know, it's where Jessie does her jumping competitions. They've got an accommodation block and . . . stuff.'

Mum looks at me. 'Disabled accommodation?'

'*Muuuuum.*'

She holds up her hands. 'All right, all right! I'm just *asking*. People who go on pony camps, they're not usually . . . I mean, do they even have the facilities you need?'

I grit my teeth. 'You said that I shouldn't see my disability as a barrier. That's what the doctors said too. You said I should be able to do everything an able-bodied person can.'

'Yes, with the necessary adaptations,' protests Mum. 'I'll look into it, all right? I'll talk to your dad and we'll ring Berry Farm and talk to them. Is it just the one night away?'

'Four. Tuesday to Saturday.'

'*Four* nights away!' Mum looks shocked.

'Everyone else is going,' I say, which isn't strictly true. Only Jessie is definitely booked on the camp so far. Summer says the charity KidzRide that provides her and Daniel's lessons for free has a fund that can be used for things like this, but she doesn't yet know if either of them will qualify. I don't know how but I just KNOW we'll all make it there somehow.

'Don't you need a pony?' asks Mum.

'I can ask Starlight to lend me one,' I say. 'Jessie says they've done it before.'

Mum looks at me, and she knows that when I'm this determined, it's very hard to stop me. After my accident, my parents didn't want me riding again. They were afraid I could hurt myself even worse.

47

The doctors said I was allowed, but Mum and Dad were too scared. I got so fed up that one day, I just opened the front door and started wheeling myself to Starlight Stables. I got quite a long way before they found me, and after that they realized that they might as well let me do what I loved because I wasn't going to give up!

'All right,' says Mum now. 'We will find a way to make it work.'

I lean across and hug her tightly. 'Thanks, Mum. I love you.'

'I love you too, sweetheart,' she says into my hair. Then she sniffs my head. 'When did we last wash your hair?'

'*Mum.*'

Parents are so *parenty*.

'So are you going?' Molly asks a few days later. We're on our way to the canteen. It's Friday and that means chip day.

'Yes,' I say firmly.

'No, I mean, have they *said* you can go?'

Molly knows me well already! 'Mum said they'll make it work,' I tell her. 'She'll probably have to come with me, because I need help with some things, but she's talking to Berry Farm about it. And Starlight – I want to borrow Elvis if they'll let me.'

Molly smiles at me. 'That's amazing. It sounds like lots of fun.'

'You should come too,' I tell her as we join the back of the queue.

'I did used to ride,' says Molly, sidestepping a kid who's barrelling towards us without looking. He trips over my wheel and swears. 'Sorry,' says Molly.

'Not your fault, his,' I tell her. 'Hey, if you ride, you should totally come!'

Molly carries my tray for me and once we've got our food we head over to an empty corner.

'You should ask your parents,' I persist, shovelling chips into my mouth.

She shakes her head violently. 'I can't.'

'Why not?'

'I don't ride any more. Dad said I couldn't.' Her face is pale and she stares down at her chips instead of up at me.

I feel puzzled. She's acting quite strangely. For a moment, my fingers itch to get out my Case Notes book. But then Jessie and Summer come up with their food and I get distracted. 'Have you booked?' asks Jessie excitedly. 'For camp?'

'Hi, Molly,' says Summer.

'Hi, Summer.'

'Totally,' I tell Jessie. 'Probably. Nearly.'

'Nearly?'

'There's some stuff to be sorted out, but it'll be fine.' I grin. 'Don't worry, I'll be there! Summer, are you going? Have you heard back from KidzRide?'

Summer beams. 'Dad just texted me. They said yes! And Daniel messaged – they're going to pay for him too!'

'Oh *wow*!' I feel a huge bubble of happiness. 'This is going to be the best week ever!'

Tues 17th October

I can't believe it's pony camp ONE WEEK TODAY,
AAAAAAHHHHH! This term is going so slooooowly. Like
the lift in the Art Block, ha ha. They fixed it but it doesn't
always work and sometimes I get stuck halfway up which is
SO EMBARRASSING.

And they STILL don't know what to do with me in PE,
so I mostly go to the library now and do homework. Dad is
putting in a Strongly Worded Complaint to the school. I wish
he wouldn't. People have mostly stopped staring at me, but
I still get stupid comments like, 'Hey, can I have a go in your
chair?' and 'You got a good mark? Wow, I didn't expect that.'
Oh, and my favourite: 'I couldn't cope if I couldn't walk; my
life would basically be over.'

People so often say stuff without *thinking* properly. I
try to brush things off most of the time, but the comments
do upset me. It's like every day is a battle to get people to
see me as a *person* and not as a freak or as someone to
feel sorry for. Why don't people realize how hurtful their

comments are? Even the ones who are trying to be funny: 'Hey, can I get a lift?' GRRRRRR.

And breathe . . .

It's so much easier at Starlight where I can just be myself. I can't wait for camp - a whole week with my besties and the horses! There was a real panic when Daniel said he couldn't come after all cos his Mum needed him to look after his brothers and sister, but then they arranged for an aunt to stay for a few days so he CAN come, yay! He works so hard, he deserves it. AND Jodie says I can take ELVIS to Berry Farm! I love, love, LOVE riding him and I get to spend five whole days with him!

# Chapter 5

As our car pulls up outside Daniel's house, I can hardly breathe with excitement. The front door opens and Daniel is there, and I wave frantically at him. He grins and waves back. Mum gets out to help carry his bag to the car – which is already stuffed with our own bags and my chair – and I can see Daniel in the doorway saying goodbye to his siblings. His little sister, Sam, is clutching his waist and sobbing into his tummy, which makes me feel very sorry indeed. Daniel is talking kindly to her, though I can't hear what he's saying, and one of the other brothers tries to peel Sam's arms off Daniel, but she cries and holds on even tighter. In the end, an older woman I don't know comes to the door and says something to Sam that encourages her to let go of her brother.

Daniel finally gets to the car and slides in next to me. 'Hey, Ellie.'

I was going to exclaim, 'Yay! We're off!' but now that I've seen how difficult it was for him to leave, it doesn't seem quite appropriate. So instead, I say, 'You OK?'

He swipes at his eyes. 'Yeah. I haven't been away before. Not for this long.' As Mum pulls away from the kerb, he glances back at his front door, where Sam is still waving tearfully, the older woman standing beside her and holding her hand. It makes *me* feel upset, so it must be a hundred times worse for Daniel.

'They'll be OK,' I say consolingly, though of course I can't know that for sure.

It seems to work though, because Daniel sniffs and coughs and sits up straighter and says, 'Yeah, they'll be fine. Aunt Jo is pretty good. I just hope the boys don't mess her around too much.'

He pulls out his phone to see the screen lighting up with a message, and gives a half-laugh. 'Toby says Sam has already stopped crying because Aunt Jo has offered her strawberries dipped in chocolate.'

'Well, there you go then,' I say, smiling at him.

'Yeah.' He takes a deep breath, puts his phone away and smiles back at me. 'Looking forward to it?'

'As if you have to ask!'

He laughs and lowers his voice. 'How many snacks did you bring?'

I lean towards him and lower my voice too so Mum can't hear. 'A whole Tesco bagful.'

'You're not to eat them all at once!' Mum calls from the driver's seat, which makes me giggle.

I haven't been to Berry Farm before, though I know Jessie and Summer have. Jessie used to compete there in showjumping before her accident. Last week she got on Angus for the first time in ages and walked him round the school for about ten minutes, which was the biggest milestone ever and we all gave her loads of hugs and cheers afterwards. I don't know how much riding she'll do at camp, but apparently the organizers are really laid-back and friendly, so she says she doesn't feel under pressure.

Berry Farm is a while away, and even before we've got there my phone is buzzing with messages from Jessie and Summer who are slightly ahead of us. Eventually, we pull on to a single-track road that winds through fields and comes to a stop at a wide parking area. Up ahead to our left is the competition arena with its cafe, and beyond that I can just see buildings behind some trees.

'We're here,' says Mum cheerfully. 'And there's Jodie with the horses, ready to be unloaded. So kind of her to offer to bring them over.'

'Are you nervous?' Daniel asks me in a low voice.

I glance at him, slightly surprised. 'Are you?'

His eyes meet mine. 'No way.'

'Me neither.'

'Cool.'

'Cool.'

Jodie has brought a horsebox from Starlight with Luna, Elvis and the horse Daniel will be riding, Onyx. Onyx is a tall dark bay with a white star on his head and one white sock. He's slightly dappled, like Luna, only he's dark brown, so I think they look like bubbles of chocolate. I said once that Onyx should be called Aero like the bubbly chocolate bar!

'Thank you so much for doing this,' Mum says to Jodie as they unload the horses. Elvis nuzzles me affectionately, while Onyx kicks at the wall of the horsebox, impatient to be out.

Summer has waited with Jodie for us to arrive and now takes Luna by the leading rein and gives her a hug. 'I missed you,' I hear her whisper to Luna. 'We're going to have the best time ever.'

'Yeah, say hi to the horse and not to me,' I tease.

'Oh, I didn't mean –' Summer looks distressed.

'I'm kidding!' I say reassuringly. 'The horses are *literally* the most important part of the week.'

'Yeah, but being with the Starlight Stables Gang is a close second,' Summer says, smiling at me.

'Excited?'

'*So* excited.'

We take the ponies round to the other side of the competition centre where there's a huge stable block and tie them up outside. Each stable has a name written on a little blackboard outside, and I grin when I see that someone has added little musical notes to Elvis's! 'That's so cool.'

'Glad you like it.' An older girl holding a clipboard is smiling at me. She's short and stocky, with freckly arms and coppery hair. For a moment, she reminds me of someone, but I can't think who. 'Are you Ellie?'

'Yep.'

'I'm loving Elvis's moustache,' she says, giving him a pat. Elvis gives a whinny and shakes his head in appreciation. 'And what a beautiful singing voice he has!'

I giggle. 'Thanks.'

'I'm Hattie,' says the girl. 'I'm one of the yard girls this week. I help Geraldine and the instructors and I do chores around the place. When you've tied Elvis up, you need to take your tack and helmet and body protector to Geraldine; she's on the other side of the stables. Then she can check it over to make sure it passes all our standards.' She hesitates. 'Would you like any help with that or are you OK to do it yourself?'

I *really* like that she doesn't automatically assume I'll need someone to do it for me. 'Thanks,' I say. 'I do need a bit of help, but I've got my mum with me.'

'Oh, fine,' she says.

'Only for the first day!' I add hastily. 'To help me get set up. After that I'll be doing all of Elvis's stuff myself.'

She grins at me. 'Parents can be useful but they're better off out of the way, right?'

'So much yes,' I say with feeling.

She laughs and moves on to say hello to Daniel.

We take all my tack around the corner and join the queue of kids waiting to have their stuff checked over. There are a lot of people here! I think Mum said there would be around twenty kids on the camp, and all the parents are still here. Lots of them stare at me of course, but I'm too busy chatting to Summer to care. 'Where's Jessie?' I ask.

'Mucking out,' answers Summer. 'She got assigned a stable that hadn't been cleaned properly.'

'Oh, that's mean,' I say. 'People should leave their stables in a decent condition.'

Geraldine, the organizer, is sitting by a picnic bench with a big display board propped up against it. There are certain high standards our equipment – hats and body protectors – has to meet, so there are posters showing pictures of the right labels and markings to look out for. There's also a list of things to check on our tack. Saddles, bridles, saddle pads – they all have stitching that can come away, and metal buckles and other parts that can become rusted or bent out of shape. If you're going to ride a 500 kg animal, it's important that you have safe and secure equipment, otherwise you could end up getting hurt.

Geraldine has a wide face with a big nose and lots of laughter lines. Her medium-length hair is scraped back into a low ponytail, but there are all these little scraggly bits escaping. Her eyes, though, are steady and quite fierce – you know when someone looks directly at you and it's like they're looking right inside your head? When she greets me, I get the impression she doesn't take any nonsense, even though to the casual observer she might look a bit scatty.

*She'd be the perfect detective in a novel*, I think to myself as she checks the equipment over, ticking it off on her sheet. She smiles at me when she's done. 'Excellent, all up to scratch. Welcome to Berry Farm.'

'Thanks,' I say.

'As you know,' she carries on, and I realize her gaze has slid up to Mum standing next to me, 'we haven't had anyone in a wheelchair on our camps before, so do let us know if there's anything you need that we haven't thought of.'

'It's wheelchair *user*,' says Mum with a cheerful smile. 'Not "in a wheelchair". Wheelchair user.'

Geraldine looks surprised. 'Oh, OK, of course. I didn't realize it mattered.'

'Don't worry,' says Mum. 'It's just one of those tiny language changes that can make a difference.'

'I'm never sure what the current jargon is,' says Geraldine with a laugh.

I have that squirmy feeling in my tummy that I get when people are talking over my head. I'm quite sure Mum and Geraldine don't mean to make me uncomfortable, but it's happening all the same.

'Hey, Ellie.' Hattie has come up. 'Shall I show you where to find all the mucking-out tools? Then you can get Elvis settled in.' She says it right to me, without even a glance at Geraldine or Mum, and I feel a rush of warmth towards her.

'Good idea,' says Geraldine. 'Once you've got your horse settled in, one of the girls will show you up to the accommodation building. Lunch will be at twelve thirty.'

'Geraldine seems nice,' comments Mum as we follow Hattie.

'Mm,' I say.

The next hour is a busy one as I prepare Elvis's stable for him with lots of nice clean shavings. The farrier comes by to check all the horses' shoes; they're going to be working hard for the next few days, so it's essential that there are no wonky shoes or loose nails.

'Hey, Summer, how are Luna's metal U's?' I call to Summer, which makes her giggle. On Summer's very first day at Starlight, she couldn't remember what horseshoes were called, so she called them 'metal U's' and we've called them that ever since. Jessie's horse, Angus, is stabled on the other side of the block near Daniel's horse, Onyx. The stables are so busy! Starlight has a lot of horses, but you don't usually have twenty of them all in the same place at the same time. It makes me feel all fizzy with excitement. Everyone here is fully focused on getting their horses settled – no one has even been up to their own rooms yet! Every now and then I glance around to look at the other ponies. Some are cobs like Elvis and some look like they're thoroughbreds. I catch a glimpse of a stunning cremello being led past – I bet she's difficult to keep clean!

'Hey, Ellie.'

I swing round at the sound of a familiar voice to see Molly standing there. For a moment, my brain almost doesn't recognize her – you know how when you only ever see someone in a particular place, you kind of don't recognize them when you see them somewhere else? It's like that. And then I go, 'OH MY GOD!' and scream with excitement, and Jessie's mum, who's within earshot, says 'Jessie' automatically because she always tells Jessie off for saying that.

Molly is beaming so widely her face is almost one huge smile. 'Surprise!'

'What are you doing here?' I can't believe it.

'I'm on pony camp.' She gestures vaguely.

'But – but . . .' I don't know what to say, my mind is stuttering with questions.

'Molly!' Summer and Jessie have come over and are hugging her. 'We didn't know you were coming!'

'It was a last-minute thing,' Molly says, with a shy shrug. 'My aunt and my mum planned it in secret and only told me yesterday. And we were late setting off this morning! We had to wait till Dad went to work.'

'Why did you have to wait for that?' I ask at the same time as Summer says, 'But you're here!' and so my question goes unanswered.

'Who are you riding?' asks Jessie.

'My cousin lent me one of her ponies,' Molly says. 'She's called Echo.'

'Your cousin is called Echo?' I ask, puzzled.

'No!' Molly laughs. 'The *horse* is called Echo. My cousin is called Hattie. Oh, look, there she is!'

I turn to see Hattie, the yard girl, waving from the far end of the yard. '*Oh!*' I say. 'Now I know who she reminded me of! It was *you*!'

'Who's this?' Daniel has joined us.

Some people hate being in crowds or with lots of people, everyone talking at once. I LOVE it. Hattie comes over and everyone tries to say hi at once and squeal over Echo, who turns out to be a darling chestnut pony. We could have stayed there chatting all day, but one of the other yard girls, Fee, comes over and reminds us we only have half an hour to get our stuff into our rooms before it's lunchtime. She's Black like me, and it's kind of nice to see another Black girl here because most of the kids I've seen so far are white.

Up in the accommodation block, Mum and I find my room for the week: a downstairs accessible room for disabled users with its own wet room and a useful grab bar above the bed. 'This is nice,' comments Mum approvingly. 'I'm just down the corridor, so if you need me for anything, just call.'

She starts taking my clothes out of my case and putting them in a drawer, and I say: 'Mum,' pointedly.

'What?'

'I can do this myself,' I tell her.

'Oh. Oh, are you sure?' I roll my eyes and she frowns. 'All right, no need to be like that. I was just trying to help.'

'I know, but I can do it.' My voice is quite tetchy now.

'Don't take that tone with me. I hope you're not going to be irritable with me all week. I'm sorry you have to have your mum around – I know it's not what you would have wanted, but I have to be here for your personal care.'

'I know that.'

'I'll stay out of your way as much as I can, but I expect you to be civil to me when I'm helping you. We've worked hard to make it possible for you to come, and I don't appreciate rudeness.'

I really, really want to be MORE rude at this – why do parents insist on hammering the point home? But I bite my lip and take a breath. Then I say, keeping my voice as calm and level as possible, 'I'm sorry. I'm just overexcited and I want to do everything myself.' Sometimes when you need to defuse a situation, it's best to say what they want you to say, even if you don't want to. It's like when the detective lulls the murderer into a false sense of security. Only Mum's not a murderer.

At least, I hope she isn't.

It works, anyway. Mum nods, mollified (isn't that a great word? It means to appease or reduce someone else's anger) and goes off to unpack her own stuff. I look around my room with a sigh. It *is* a nice room, but I can't help wishing that I was with the others. Summer, Jessie and Molly are all in twin or triple rooms upstairs and I just know they're going to stay up chatting and have midnight feasts and all the things you can do when you share a room with friends. In this room there's just me.

I straighten my shoulders and start unpacking. If there's one thing I know, it's that I never let my disability get in the way of my joining in the fun and mischief. If there's out-of-hours fun to be had, I'll find a way to take part!

**@starlightstablesyouth** Hi, Starlight fans! Here's a photo of me at Berry Farm where I'm at pony camp for the week with my Gang besties! We've settled in the ponies and are sorting our rooms – look at my PALACE of a room, all just for me! Aren't I lucky? Lunch soon and I'm starving – what are YOU having for lunch today? Don't forget to hit follow so you don't miss any camp fun updates!
Love Ellie xxx

**#horsesaremylife #ilovehorses
#ponymad #starlightstablesgang #ssg**

# Chapter 6

Over lunch, we have a talk from Geraldine and the other staff. She introduces us to the instructors, the yard girls (four of them including Hattie and Fee) and two mums who are going to be staying in the accommodation block with us overnight.

'Where do the yard girls sleep?' I ask Jessie in a whisper.

'In a horsebox down by the stables,' she whispers back.

'In a *horsebox*?!' repeats Summer, shocked.

Jessie giggles. 'Yeah, one of those big ones with fold-down beds. It's amazing. I totally want to be a yard girl when I'm older. They sleep right by the horses to keep an eye on them overnight. And they don't have to go to bed on time!'

I'm impressed. That sounds like a fun thing to do, actually. It's basically like a prolonged sleepover – with horses!

'Shh,' says Fee, shooting us a look.

I don't know how I'm going to remember all the names, so I slide my Case Notes book out of my bag and start scribbling.

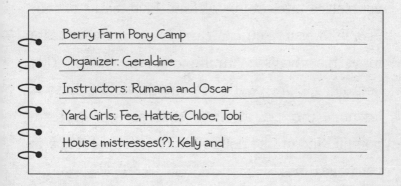

Berry Farm Pony Camp

Organizer: Geraldine

Instructors: Rumana and Oscar

Yard Girls: Fee, Hattie, Chloe, Tobi

House mistresses(?): Kelly and

'Who was the second house lady thingy?' I ask Jessie.

'Um . . . Nina? I think.'

'Shh,' says Fee again, more loudly this time, and a girl with a little snub nose and long brown hair in a French plait turns round to glare at us. She looks about my age, and I glare back at her. Her blue eyes narrow and her lips press together tightly.

'*What?*' I hiss at her, and she turns away, wrinkling her nose as though I smell bad.

Summer and I exchange a look. Everyone is so nice at Starlight, I sometimes forget that not all riders are the same!

'We're also running a team competition during camp,' Geraldine says, and a frisson of excitement passes through the room. 'I need you to get yourselves into groups of four. Five teams of four people in each. You can earn points for your team in various ways. Winning quizzes, having tidy bedrooms, being neatly presented, working hard in lessons – these are all things that can earn you team points. Kind of like house points at school if any of you have those.'

Jessie puts up her hand. 'Can we have five people in our team?'

'No, I'm sorry,' says Geraldine firmly. 'Only four. You've got two minutes to decide on your teams.'

The four members of the Starlight Stables Gang and Molly look at each other. 'I'll go join another group,' offers Daniel, starting to get up.

'No!' I say sharply. 'No, you can't, you're in our team.'

'But what about Molly?'

There's an agonized moment where none of us knows what to say. And then Molly says, 'It's fine. You're a gang already.' She bites her lip and gets up, looking around like a lost puppy.

'Ellie,' Jessie hisses at me. 'We can't kick Molly out.'

'I told you, I'll go —' Daniel starts to get up again.

'Sit down,' I snap at him. 'You can't go.'

'But poor Molly,' says Summer, looking distressed. 'I could go join another . . .' She trails off. Summer is probably the least confident of all of us.

Maybe I should offer to pair up with Molly and then find another pair to make a team? And then the other SSG members could find an extra person? I'm still dithering over suggesting this when the French Plait Girl at the next table turns round and says to Molly, 'Are you spare? We need another person.'

'Oh, thanks,' says Molly gratefully, and I feel AWFUL. You know when you have so many different emotions at once that you kind of feel a bit sick? I feel so happy the four of us are in a team, but gutted that Molly isn't with us, and sorry for her because I already don't like French Plait Girl.

'Everyone sorted?' calls Geraldine. 'Right, the yard girls are coming round with ribbons in the team colours. Make sure you're wearing your team ribbon every day and it's clearly visible. Tie it to your hat or around your upper arm – somewhere everyone can see it. You don't want to miss out on valuable points! Every evening at dinner, I'll read out how many points each team has earned, and there's a chart outside the canteen where stickers will be added. At the end of the week, the winning team gets a trophy.'

Hattie comes round and hands us four blue ribbons. Molly's group gets red. I tie a quick release knot in mine and slip it round my wrist. The others do the same.

'A trophy!' says Jessie. 'We *have* to win!'

I glance around the room and I'm willing to bet that every other person is thinking the same thing.

After lunch is over, everyone has to wash up their own plate and cutlery in a bowl at the end of the table. 'I'll do yours,' I offer to Summer, who's wriggling and complaining she needs the loo.

'Are you sure?'

'Yep, no problem.'

'Thank you!' She dashes off.

Speaking of the toilet, I realize after I've washed up our things that it's time for me to go too. 'I'll wait for you,' offers Daniel, which is really nice of him since nearly everyone has headed back outside. We're going to tack up and do some flatwork in the arena so that the instructors can assess our riding ability and work out which groups to put us in.

'Oh, no,' I say, 'you don't have to.'

'I don't mind.'

'No, I mean it,' I say, and I can feel my face burning in embarrassment. Unlike other people, going to the toilet takes me AGES. See, it's not an easy thing to 'go' when you can't feel anything in that area. I usually take about half an hour just for a wee. It's a very complicated process, involving tubes and things, and everything has to be CLEAN CLEAN CLEAN because I could get an infection and not realize. But obviously I'm not going to tell Daniel all that – can you imagine?! So instead I say, 'Honestly, that's really nice of you but . . . um . . . I take ages in the loo, so I'll see you down at the stables afterwards.'

'Oh, OK,' he says, and lopes off. Daniel never makes a fuss about anything; it's one of the reasons I like him.

When I first had my accident, Mum and Dad had to do all my toileting stuff for me, but now I can manage some of it myself. After I'm done, I head down to the stables, where most of the horses are already tacked up. 'Hey, Ellie,' says Hattie, smiling at me. 'Everything OK?'

'Yep.'

She hesitates. 'Um, no one has told me how . . . how you get up on to Elvis. Do you . . . um . . .'

'Oh,' I say. 'I'm going to be lifted. At Starlight I use a hoist, but Geraldine said they don't have one here, so someone will lift me.'

Hattie looks relieved. 'Oh, fine! I'll get Geraldine.'

I give Elvis a quick brush down and then tack him up. He's such a good boy, bending down so I can slip the bridle over his ears. Carmen would never help out like that!

Geraldine lifts me out of my chair and then walks up the mounting block and places me in the saddle. 'All right?' she says, slipping my feet into the stirrups.

'Yep,' I say. 'Can you put these on for me too?' I hold out the elastic bands. 'They stop my feet slipping out as I ride.'

I'm the last one to join the group, but it doesn't matter because they're taking it in turns to ride anyway. I don't think I've ever seen twenty children on twenty horses all in the same place at the same time! It's kind of exciting. Molly waves at me from further up the queue. Daniel, astride Onyx, has hung back and now says, 'All right, slowcoach?' with a grin. I stick my tongue out at him and grin back.

In pairs, we go into the arena and the two instructors, Rumana and Oscar, watch us ride in circles and on diagonals, trotting if we can, cantering if we're more confident. Then they have a quick chat with each rider to find out their strengths and weaknesses and whether their pony has any particular quirks they should know about. It makes me glad again that I haven't brought Carmen. She's an amazing pony but she's scared of hedges, would you believe? Long, swooshy grass, rustling hedges – I don't know what she thinks is going to happen, but she won't go anywhere near them, which means you can't take her out on hacks in the countryside.

On horseback, I look like everyone else, and I love it. Up here, I don't instantly stand out as different. Hattie and Fee and the other yard girls encourage us

to clap and cheer each other as we finish in the arena. The French Plait Girl from earlier is now wearing a neon pink hat silk and riding a beautiful little grey. She canters super-fast around the arena, but she looks awfully bouncy in the saddle. Despite that, she grins smugly at everyone as she goes past, as if to say, 'Look at me, aren't I amazing?' She's not all that.

Jessie and Angus go next, and my heart squeezes looking at her plod slowly round in a circle. I can tell she's controlling her breathing and trying to remain calm. Not so long ago, she could have raced around like French Plait Girl (though Jessie rides way more smoothly!), but it's taking a long time to battle her anxiety. Oscar, the instructor watching her, calls out lots of very encouraging things, and when eventually she comes to a halt, he goes over and talks to her in a low, reassuring tone. Even though her hands are shaking, she smiles back at him and nods.

Summer, Daniel, Molly and I cheer VERY loudly when Jessie comes out of the arena.

There's a real range of ability here: some kids are absolutely amazing, zooming around like rockets; others are clearly very much beginners, not yet confident at shortening or lengthening the rein. Summer says gloomily as a little boy zips round the arena, 'He's so much better than me, and he's *younger* too!'

'Stop it,' I say firmly to her. 'There's nothing wrong with starting riding later. Some people don't start riding till they're grown up! And everyone progresses at different rates. Don't compare yourself to others.'

She smiles at me. 'Thanks, Ellie. You're so right.'

Summer worries that she's not good enough, but riding isn't about being the best; it's about the relationship between horse and rider and doing something together.

I'm so busy thinking about this that I miss my name being called, and Summer has to repeat it. I touch Elvis gently with the whips and he moves forward. Rumana comes to meet me, smiling. 'Hi, you must be Ellie. We're going to start off nice and gentle, with some twenty-metre circles – that OK?'

'No problem.'

Elvis is a DARLING, as expected, and I can't help feeling a little pleased at the surprised looks from some of the other riders. I bet loads of them have never even seen a wheelchair user on a horse, and it's kind of cool that I can show them I'm no different from the rest of them. French Plait Girl looks as though she's smelled something bad again. I definitely don't like her!

'Lovely work,' says Rumana, coming towards me with a smile. 'So tell me about your riding experience, Ellie. Do you jump? Cross-country? Dressage?'

I plunge into a list of all my riding ambitions, and Rumana listens carefully and asks a few more questions before saying she's got enough to go on. As I exit the arena, a couple of the kids give me impressed nods, and I beam back at them. French Plait Girl blanks me entirely. She reminds me of the snobby Head Girl in a mystery book I read, who told the heroine she was wasting her time investigating a murder. The heroine proved her wrong in the end, of course!

'Right,' Rumana calls to all of us. 'We'd like you all back in the arena, going large – that means walking nice and gently round the edge. No trotting or cantering, and no overtaking unless the horse in front of you has stopped to do its business, OK?'

We all turn our ponies back into the arena and do as directed, while Rumana and Oscar stand together and discuss who should be in which group.

'And everyone stop!' calls Oscar after three circuits. 'That's great, thank you all very much. So Rumana and I have settled on the two groups. In my group will be . . .' He rattles off a list of names, none of which I know.

'And in my group,' says Rumana, 'the following: Jessie, Summer, Finn, Luke, Daniel, Molly, Tanya, Ellie, Annabel and Kizzy. Can you all put your hands up for me?'

Yesss, we're all together! I beam at Molly in her red ribbon and my blue team SSG buddies, who are all grinning back at me.

Then I realize French Plait Girl has her hand up too, and my jaw drops in annoyance. She glares at me and I glare back. Typical! Why do I have to have the horrible girl in my group?!

'That's enough for the first day,' says Rumana. 'We're all going to head back and untack and then I think Geraldine has some group activities planned.'

'Aww,' says Daniel, sounding disappointed. 'No more riding today?'

Oscar hears him and laughs. 'Don't worry, by the time we get to the end of the week, your bottom will be sore from the saddle!'

←

**@starlightstablesyouth** Hi SSG fans! Here's a photo of me and Summer on Elvis and Luna – don't the ponies look gorgeous? The first day is FLYING by! After our first riding session, we were each given a sheet of random images. We had to work out what they were and then find the real thing around the yard. Some of them, like the wheelbarrows, were easy to spot, but one of the photos was REALLY hard and in the end I gave up. It turned out to be a close-up of a stirrup, but only about three people recognized it! We all felt so embarrassed! Dinner now and then THE BIG QUIZ, yay! Wish the SSG team luck!

**#horsesaremylife #ilovehorses #ponymad #starlightstablesgang #ssg #berryfarm #ponycamp**

# Chapter 7

I feel a bit bad when I see Molly going to sit with the red team for the quiz after dinner. She doesn't say anything, but her face falls when we head into the lounge and the tables are set up in the team colours. French Plait Girl, who turns out to be Tanya, is already there, chatting away to the two other girls in their team. When Molly sits down, Tanya barely seems to notice her. Molly folds her hands in her lap and stays quiet and I feel guilty all over again. I'm about to wheel myself over to see if she's OK when I see that Hattie, the yard girl and Molly's cousin, has got there before me. She puts a hand on Molly's shoulder and bends down to say something. Molly shakes her head violently, and Hattie sighs and moves on.

'I feel really sorry for Molly,' I whisper to Summer.

She follows my gaze. 'Oh no, why does she look so sad?'

'That horrible Tanya is basically blanking her.'

'I'm sure she's not doing it on purpose.' Summer is still trying to see the best in people. 'Maybe she was already friends with the other two in her team? You know what it's like when someone new joins your group.'

'Huh,' I say, not prepared to give Tanya the benefit of the doubt.

Geraldine, the organizer, is at the front and is one of those people who only has to stand and wait for everyone else to fall silent. The head teacher at my primary school was like that. 'Good evening, everyone, and welcome to our quiz! You'll have noticed that I didn't read out the team points at dinner earlier. That's because whichever team wins the quiz will also win four points, one for each member of their team. So I'll read out today's team points at the end of the quiz. Now, on each of your tables is a set of answer papers and a pen. You need to choose a person in each team who will write the answers, so choose the one with the neatest handwriting.'

'That's you,' Daniel says to me.

'No, it's Summer,' I say.

Summer shakes her head. 'I don't mind, you do it.'

'Question one,' says Geraldine, making me scrabble to pick up the pen. 'Name the part of the horse where the mane meets the back.'

'Withers,' Jessie whispers urgently.

'Shhh!' I say. 'Don't let the others hear!'

'Question two. What are the three events in three-day eventing?'

We all grin at each other. We know exactly what they are because we went to watch eventing at Haversham Horse Trials! I write down, 'Cross-country, dressage and showjumping'.

'Question three. Name the British para-equestrian who holds *six* gold Paralympic medals.'

The room, which has been filled with excited mutterings and rustlings, suddenly falls silent as the riders look blankly at each other. But I know this one – how could I not?! She's a role model for disabled riders everywhere! Grinning at my teammates, I write, 'Natasha Baker'.

'Nice one, Ellie,' whispers Daniel.

I glance up to see Tanya staring in my direction. I raise my eyebrows and she screws up her face and turns away. Honestly, what is her problem?!

The questions continue. Some of them are easy: 'What's it called when a horse stops dead at a jump?' (Refusal.) 'What's the piece of metal called that goes in the horse's mouth?' (The bit.) Others are harder. 'If your horse is known to kick, what should it wear in competitions to warn the other riders?' (Luckily Jessie knows this one: it's a red ribbon in the tail.) 'What part of a horse would a princess kiss?' (We all stare at each other blankly. 'Why would a princess kiss a horse?' asks Daniel. 'Write down nose, because that's the only part I kiss,' suggests Jessie.)

There's a picture round where we have to identify the colour of each horse. Jessie and Daniel get into an argument about the differences between piebald, skewbald, flea-bitten and paint horse. And Summer insists that palominos can't have white manes. From the rise in noise during this round, it sounds like other teams are arguing too!

Eventually, the quiz is over and we hand in all the answer sheets. 'Well done, everyone,' says Geraldine. 'Hattie and Fee are going to mark these while we all go down to the stables to do our last check on the ponies. Skip out, turn out those that need to be in the fields overnight. Half an hour tops, then straight back here for the results, all right? No dawdling!'

'My gosh, it's half past seven already,' gasps Summer. 'Where did the day go?'

I'm suddenly terribly tired. The thought of going back down to the stables is kind of daunting. The others are all getting up and heading out of the door. Only Daniel hesitates. 'You all right, Ellie?'

'Yeah,' I say, not feeling all right at all. 'I'm fine.'

'Listen,' he says. 'I know you don't want any help, but would you like me to go check on Elvis for you? I bet your arms are worn out from wheeling around today.'

Actually, my whole body aches, not just my arms. Normally by this point of the day at home, I'm slumped on the sofa watching TV, not skipping out a pony. I bite my lip. I *hate* accepting help, but I know sometimes I need it, and this is probably one of those times. 'That would be nice, if you don't mind,' I say, wishing that I could just run along like everyone else.

He smiles at me. 'No problem. I'll make sure he's set up for the night.'

Daniel is SO nice. As he heads out of the door, Nina, one of the house parents, comes over to me. 'Hey, Ellie, we haven't properly met. I'm Nina. You a bit worn-out? Your mum said you might be by now.'

Instantly, I wish I'd gone down to the stables to prove my mum wrong!

'She's been working in the conference room today,' says Nina. 'Shall I pop to fetch her?'

I scowl. 'I suppose so.'

Nina looks at me sympathetically. 'Bit of a pain to have your mum around, I guess? You should talk to my daughter, Skye. She finds me *terribly* embarrassing. You OK to stay here while I go fetch your mum?'

I nod and she disappears. I am left sitting alone in the empty room, staring at the comfy chairs, the round tables, the blue carpet, and listening to ... nothing. Pony camp is going to be great, I know it is. But I guess you can't love every single second of something.

Mum gives me a big hug when she comes in, and absurdly, I really want to burst into tears. 'Had a good time?' she asks, and I nod, unable to speak. 'I've been working in this little conference room,' she goes on. 'But every now and then I'd get up and have a bit of a wander, stretch my legs a bit. I saw you a couple of times down at the stables and in the arena. You looked like you were doing *brilliantly*. I'm so proud of you.'

That sets me off properly, and the tears stream down my face. I hug her even tighter, and she hugs me back.

'Oh, Ellie, what's happened? Has someone said something nasty?'

'No,' I sob. 'Everyone's been fine. Except this girl called Tanya; she looked at me funny.'

Mum chuckles softly. 'Looked at you funny?' She gets a pack of tissues out of her bag and hands me one. 'Big day, huh?'

'Yeah, I guess.'

She pauses for a moment and then says, 'You know, this is the biggest adventure you've been on since your accident. I mean, we've been on holiday and things like that, but your dad and I have always been right there next to you.'

I roll my damp eyes. 'Yeah, *right* next to me.'

She laughs again. 'I know, I know – overprotective, you keep saying. But here – well, you don't want me next to you the whole time. You're growing up. Changing schools was a big step. This is another one. You know I can be around more if you want. You don't have to do everything yourself – riding is physically exhausting anyway, and you're doing mucking out and tacking up and all kinds of other activities.'

I shake my head. 'I want to do it all myself. I don't want anyone to feel sorry for me. I just . . . I'm just a bit tired, that's all.'

She nods. 'Well, I don't suppose they'll be much longer out there. I know when everyone comes back up you're going to have hot chocolate and cake while they announce the winners of the quiz.'

'Cake before bed?!' I say, cheering up instantly.

'Don't get any ideas,' she warns. 'This is just for pony camp, when everyone's using up lots of energy. After that, I'll help you get settled in bed.'

I know my room is a bit isolated and I might feel a bit lonely, but at the moment, the idea of lying down on a soft mattress and pillow is *really* appealing!

---

Tues 24<sup>th</sup> October

I am so pooped I can hardly keep my eyes open. We didn't win the quiz (a princess would kiss the FROG! That was such a clever question; I'm so annoyed we didn't guess it. The underside of a horse's hoof is called a frog). We came joint third, which was all right. The red team with Tanya in it won by half a point – she was SOOOOOOOO smug about it.

---

Molly looked happy though, so I was pleased for her. She said it was mostly the others in the team who knew the answers and that she felt useless, but I said not to be silly. Besides, they won, so it didn't matter who knew the answers and who didn't, right? On the way out, Hattie said to Molly: 'See, it was worth coming, wasn't it?' and Molly smiled and said she guessed so.

Geraldine read out the team points and surprise, surprise, the red team is in the lead. We've got some catching up to do!

Daniel was so kind this evening. He said he turned Elvis out into the field with Onyx and they went off together. (Aww, our ponies are bonding!) He also skipped out Elvis's stable so I won't have to do it in the morning.

I feel a bit silly about crying earlier. I think everything just got on top of me. Mum says it's good to cry, but I don't like it. I felt better after hot chocolate and cake. Battenberg is disgusting, by the way. It's got pink and yellow squares inside it, so it looks pretty, but the icing tastes of marzipan. YUCK. I swallowed it quickly and had a big gulp of hot chocolate to take away the taste. Then I had a chocolate mini roll. And a Viennese Whirl.

Jessie, Summer and Daniel have been messaging me from upstairs. J and S are in a room together. Daniel is sharing with two other boys called Finn and Luke. I wish there was someone else in my room. Not my mum!!! She's down the corridor.

I'm so tired. Sleep now! Tomorrow there will be RIDING, SO MUCH RIDING zzzzzzz

# Chapter 8

I'm fast asleep when Mum comes in the next morning, but I wake up very quickly. Today is the first full day at pony camp! After I do washing and use the toilet and all that boring stuff, I get dressed and do my hair. Riding helmets mean you can't do anything fancy with your hair or wear clips because they can dig into your head and the helmet wouldn't fit properly. But I've got some hair chalks with me, so I get out the blue one and put some long blue streaks in my hair – go, blue team!

I'm just finishing up when Summer and Jessie come and knock on my door. 'Your hair looks *amazing*!' says Jessie. 'Can you do mine as well?'

'And mine,' says Summer.

We're nearly late for breakfast, but it's worth it to see Tanya's face as we come into the canteen and she sees what we've done. Her eyes widen as she sees our matching hair and I can just tell she's REALLY jealous! As we pass, she turns to one of the girls she's with and says in a low tone, 'Have any of you got hair chalks?', but they shake their heads and I want to laugh.

Molly is sitting on her own, so we go to join her once we've got our food. Breakfast is way more impressive than the one I get at home. Bacon, eggs, sausages, mushrooms, tomatoes, hash browns – even black pudding, which I tried once and liked, but then Dad told me what was in it, and I nearly turned vegetarian. Daniel comes in shortly afterwards and he has *two* slices of black pudding, and I go off him a bit.

Nina and Kelly are serving up the breakfasts, and my mum is helping them in the kitchen. The yard girls come to eat, chattering and laughing about something, and the noise in the canteen gradually reaches epic excited proportions.

Geraldine calls for silence near the end. 'The schedule for the week has been put up on the board just outside the canteen,' she says. 'Please have a look at it and make a note of where you need to be at what time. Remember, your ponies are your responsibility all the time you're here – except for overnight, when the yard girls will be in charge. But at all other times, you need to be looking after them, and there will always be work to do around the stables. If you have any concerns about your horse, please let me or one of the instructors know immediately.' She smiles. 'And let's have some fun! Today's schedule is packed with activities. When you're not riding, you'll either be doing stable chores under the eye of the yard girls or taking part in a non-riding activity. Remember, you can earn points for your team throughout the day!'

After we've washed up our plates and cutlery again, we all stream out of the canteen. There's such a crush of people looking at the schedule on the board, it takes ages before I can get to see it. Craning my neck upwards, I see that Rumana's riding group will be starting with flatwork in the arena (which is practising the basics without any poles or obstacles) while Oscar's will be out on cross-country. And there's a group activity to do too, something called 'tower building'.

'I wonder what that is,' says Summer curiously.

'Look.' Jessie nods towards the team chart next to the schedule. Yesterday's points have been added to the chart and we can see six stickers in the blue row and eight in the red. 'Five for yellow, six for green and purple. The teams are so close at the moment – we have to keep earning those points!'

'That's right,' says Nina, overhearing her. She smiles at me. 'Feeling a bit better this morning?'

'Definitely,' I tell her.

'That's great. Top tip: I'll be awarding points for neat and tidy bedrooms, and I'm heading there in *ten minutes* . . .'

We all squeal and dash back to the accommodation block. My heart sinks at the sight of my room: I'm *so* not a tidy person. 'Muuuum!' I yell, but there's no answer. She did say she was going to start work after breakfast, so I guess she must be back in the conference room. Bother! I do the best I can in the couple of minutes I have before we all have to head down to the stables. I'd rather earn points for my riding than my bedroom anyway.

At the stables, the horses have all been fed and watered by the yard girls. Elvis nickers when he sees me and puts his head down so I can stroke his nose. 'Aww,' I say. 'Hello, Elvis. Ready to do some work? It's a bit chilly today, isn't it?'

I've never had a lesson with my Gang friends before and it is *so* much fun – and I'm really glad Molly is with us! Her pony, Echo, is very docile, and Molly sometimes has to get quite bossy before Echo will move into a trot. Rumana keeps telling

Molly she needs to be more commanding, but I'm not sure Molly's a commanding sort of person. I think Jessie must have explained about her anxiety to Rumana yesterday because she does everything at a walk and Rumana doesn't even suggest she go any faster. Elvis is PERFECTION, obviously.

The only annoying thing is Tanya. She behaves as if she knows everything – she tells me to shorten my reins! Me!! – but she can't even control her *own* pony, Silver. Silver tosses his head a lot and skips sideways and keeps trying to overtake the pony in front – and Tanya makes a lot of noise, saying, 'Oh, *Silver*,' but not properly taking control. Rumana calls out encouraging things like, 'Try not to lean back, Tanya,' and, 'Try to give nice clear signals to Silver, Tanya,' and Tanya just carries on doing the same things.

Overall, though, Rumana seems pleased. 'I'm awarding two team points,' she says as we finish up. 'Jessie, you can have a point for staying calm and solid in the saddle – well done.'

Jessie beams. Tanya leans forward in anticipation, but Rumana continues with, 'And, Daniel, you can have a point for that beautifully smooth change of rein you did in the middle. You're both on the blue team, I see. Good work!'

Tanya puts up her hand. 'Did I do a good change of rein, Rumana?'

'Not bad,' Rumana tells her. 'It could be a bit smoother though, Tanya. Just keep working on those core muscles!' She turns away. 'Time to head back. Everyone dismount – except you, Ellie, you can ride back to the stables – and make sure you all give your ponies a good rub-down and a hay net. We've made a great start – well done, everyone!'

From my position still on Elvis, I think I'm the only one to see Tanya shoot Daniel a dark look as they dismount. So not only is Tanya a show-off, she's also a sore loser!

Molly looks a little disappointed as we head back to the stables. 'Don't worry,' I hear Summer say to her. 'You did brilliantly.'

'I haven't ridden much,' Molly says. 'You guys have had loads more experience.'

'Not me!' says Summer. 'I only started riding a few months ago. Don't put yourself down – that's what the others keep telling me.'

Tobi and Hattie are waiting for us at the stables. 'How did it go?' asks Tobi cheerfully.

'Great!' I tell her, beaming. 'Is Geraldine around to help me down?'

'Is it OK if I help you?' Tobi asks. 'Geraldine and your mum gave me a lesson.'

'Yep, that's fine,' I say.

'Let me know if I do it wrong,' Tobi says. She's tall and strong-looking with long brown hair streaked with pink.

'Perfect,' I say as she puts me gently in my chair. 'Thanks, Tobi.'

'Any time. I'll try to make sure I'm around for the beginning and end of your lessons – and just shout for me if I'm not.'

'Thanks!' I give Elvis a pat before reaching to

unbuckle the girth. 'You were a good boy, weren't you, Elvis? Can't wait for the hack this afternoon.'

We start our stable chores under the watchful eyes of Tobi and Hattie, who make sure we do everything correctly and in the right order. Molly forgets to run up her stirrups before taking off the saddle, so Hattie makes her do it again. I hear her saying to Molly, 'It's all right, don't beat yourself up. Everyone makes mistakes.' I fetch a fork and skip out Elvis's stable. The yard girls brought him in early this morning and he's already pooed in it twice! It's a good thing the stable doors are nice and wide – my wheelchair slides through the gap no problem.

The riders from Oscar's group clatter into the stables, enthusing loudly about the cross-country. 'OK?' a boy asks Jessie as he passes.

'Hey, Rio. Yeah, good. What's the cross-country like?'

'Awesome. Some amazing jumps.'

Jessie gulps as Rio leads his horse round the corner.

'Don't worry,' says Hattie, overhearing. 'Your group probably won't be doing the jumps. You can always go round them anyway.'

'Team points available for a clean stable and horse!' Tobi calls from the end of the yard. 'I'm coming round in just a minute!'

'Argh!' Jessie dashes off to the other side of the block.

Quickly, I move round to Elvis's tail to give it a thorough brush. I did it earlier, but it's already tangled again. I'm still brushing when I hear Tobi coming, Daniel trailing behind her protesting.

'He was completely clean a few minutes ago, I promise!'

'You must have missed a bit,' says Tobi, giving a shrug.

'I didn't!'

I look round. 'What's going on?'

'Right, let's have a look at Elvis,' says Tobi, running her hand down his neck.

Daniel is upset. 'He was neat as anything a minute ago,' he says again.

'I'm sorry, Daniel, I can't give you a point if he's not clean when I see him,' says Tobi, sounding sympathetic but firm. 'There was a big patch of mud on his left flank – you must have groomed him in too much of a hurry.'

'I didn't!' Furious now, Daniel kicks at a nearby stable door. I bite my lip. Daniel hates being accused of something he didn't do.

'Hey!' Tobi straightens up, sharp. 'Don't you lose your temper with me. Was there or was there not a patch of mud on Onyx's flank?'

Daniel scowls at the ground.

Tobi folds her arms. She's much taller than Daniel and she doesn't look impressed. 'Well?'

Daniel squirms, wretched, and I feel sorry for him. 'There was.'

'Right. So you don't get a point. That's all. No big deal. You can earn loads more as the day goes on.' Tobi returns her attention to Elvis and nods in satisfaction. 'Lovely job, Ellie. What's your team colour?'

'Blue.' I show her the ribbon.

'Excellent. I'll make a note and tell Geraldine.' She raises her voice. 'Summer, I'm coming to look at your horse now!' She heads towards Luna, and I swing round to see Daniel stomping off in the other direction.

Daniel does have a bit of a temper, but I'm really surprised at the way he's behaving. Quickly, I persuade Elvis into his stable and make sure he can reach the hay net I hung in there earlier. Then I do up the bolts and wheel myself round the corner after Daniel.

He's standing by Onyx, his forehead leaning against the pony's, his eyes closed. He looks like he's trying to calm down. 'Daniel?' I ask. 'What's the matter, what happened?'

'Oh, hey, Ellie.' He doesn't look at me. 'It's stupid. I don't know. But I don't understand it.'

'Understand what?'

He sighs and pulls back from Onyx. 'I groomed him before the lesson. Really well. You know I do a good job.'

'Yeah?'

'And I did him afterwards too. He didn't have a scrap of mud on him, I swear. I was gone for maybe two minutes while I was fetching a new hay net. When I got back, he had this big lump of mud on his left side. All stuck in his coat. I've brushed it out now. But I can't work out how it got there – I mean, where from?' He gestures at our surroundings. There's the stable block, and the concrete outside, and a few cracks in the paving and – yes – some patches of dirt.

'He couldn't have rolled?' I ask doubtfully.

'How? He was tied up. I just don't get it, Ellie. It was like – like someone had just got a handful of mud and slapped it on him – just here.' He points. Onyx flicks his ears as if agreeing.

I hesitate. 'What if someone did?'

His eyes meet mine. 'Surely not.' But his voice is quieter. 'Why would anyone do that?'

Instantly, my mind flashes back to what I saw in the arena at the end of the lesson: Tanya's glare. 'Maybe someone didn't like you winning a team point.'

'That's ridiculous. Who would be that annoyed?'

I press my lips together. I don't want to accuse Tanya of something she might not have done. But surely she's the most likely person?

Daniel looks down at his hands and then back up at me. His eyes look thoughtful. 'Ellie, you know we sometimes make fun of your Case Notes book . . .'

I beam at him. 'Are you asking me to open a case file on the mud on Onyx?'

'Well – not exactly – but . . . maybe? It just seems so odd.'

I reach behind me for the bag on the back of my chair. 'I am *on* it.'

He nods. 'Thanks, Ellie.'

I head to the end of the building and take a quick glance round to see that no one is watching me. Then I start scribbling.

Case #24: Onyx's Mud

Location: stables at Berry Farm

Date: Tuesday 24th October

Time: 11.03 a.m.


In brief: Daniel groomed Onyx. Was absent for two

minutes. Returned to find patch of mud on M's left

flank.

How? Who? Why?


Prime Suspect: Tanya

Tanya wanted a team point in the lesson and didn't

get one. She was angry that Daniel *did* get a point. Could

she have run up to Onyx while Daniel was fetching the

hay net and rubbed mud into Onyx?

'Ellie.' Hattie is coming towards me, so I hastily stuff the Case Notes back in my bag. 'What's that?'

'Nothing.'

'We've got an activity for you all to do,' she says, smiling. 'You can earn more points for your team . . .'

'I'm there!'

The team activity turns out to be a crazy engineering thing where we have to design and build the tallest tower possible using only dried spaghetti and marshmallows. Five tables are set up on the lawn outside the accommodation block, each labelled with a colour for the teams.

'Oh, I love this kind of thing,' exclaims Summer.

'I did this at school once,' says Daniel. 'Did you know the strongest shape for building is a triangle?'

Tanya, standing at the next table, immediately bends forward and whispers to her teammates, 'We need to make triangles.'

'Hey!' I say, annoyed. 'Stop listening in!'

'It's a free country,' says Tanya over her shoulder.

'Can you *believe* her?' I say to the gang in a low voice.

'Don't worry,' says Daniel. 'We've totally got this.' He starts explaining how to snap the spaghetti into regular lengths and stick three pieces into three marshmallows in an equilateral triangle. 'If we make loads, we can then start stacking them. Like the Eiffel Tower. That's made out of triangles.'

'What's this got to do with horses?' moans Jessie, casting a longing glance over to the stable block.

'Nothing,' say Daniel. 'But it's got everything to do with points.'

'OH,' says Jessie, snapping to attention. '*Now* I'm interested.'

Between the four of us, under Daniel's instruction, we build an impressive tower. When the time's up and the yard girls come round to measure the results, the blue team wins by *miles*.

'This is amazing,' says Hattie, shaking her head in awe. 'It looks like the Eiffel Tower!'

We all exchange smug glances.

Despite the efforts of the red team to copy us, their tower is a full eighteen centimetres shorter than ours. Tanya is clearly cross. 'It's your fault,' I hear her say to Molly. 'You didn't make the original triangles big enough.'

'You didn't tell me what size to make them,' Molly objects.

'Couldn't you use your eyes and see what everyone else was doing?' hisses Tanya.

Molly falls silent, her face red, and I have *very angry feelings* towards Tanya. As soon as the yard girls declare us the winner and say we'll be getting team points, everyone disperses and Molly comes over to us. 'It wasn't your fault,' I tell her firmly.

She shrugs, looking miserable. 'They should have done it without me. I wasn't any help anyway.'

'They're not being a good team,' I tell her, frustrated. 'They're not including you properly. Tanya seems to be running a dictatorship.'

'I don't know what that means.'

'Have a marshmallow,' Daniel offers, holding out the bag which contains considerably fewer marshmallows than it did. 'It's cheered me up, winning a point! Makes up for the point I didn't get for grooming Onyx.'

'Why didn't you get a point?' asks Jessie, and Daniel explains about the mud.

'Ellie thinks maybe someone did it on purpose,' he finishes.

'Oh no!' Summer is shocked. 'I can't believe anyone would be that mean.'

But I can easily believe it. There are all kinds of people in the world, and some of them are definitely mean.

# Chapter 9

The afternoon hack is FUN! The earlier chilliness has worn off and the sun comes out, and we set off down a narrow path between hedges (again, thank goodness I didn't bring Carmen): all ten of us in Rumana's group along with Rumana herself on a gorgeous black mare, and Hattie and Fee on their own ponies.

Jessie wasn't at all sure she wanted to come at first. She had a bit of an anxiety wobble as we were setting off, but Hattie and Summer talked her round and she agreed to come as long as she could ride next to one of them.

The end of the path opens on to a wide stretch of grassland, dotted with scrubby bushes. The horses fan out, no longer confined to single file, and I take a deep breath. 'Remember this is the bit I warned you all about!' shouts Rumana from the front. 'Don't let your pony speed up! Walking only for the moment!'

It's a timely reminder because I can feel Elvis's movement change and his head pull forward, keen to move into a canter. 'No,' I tell him, pulling gently back. 'Walk, Elvis.' He does so, obediently. To my right, Onyx skips and prances, suddenly excited at all the open space. I'm about to call advice to Daniel, suggest he pulls Onyx up, but then I realize he's started talking to the pony in a low, calm voice.

'It's all right, boy, I know you're excited. It looks like fun, doesn't it? But we can't go dashing off because we're part of a group, and the group sticks together. Nice and gentle, Onyx, there you go. Nice and calm.'

My jaw drops as the pony stops skipping about and relaxes back into a walk. Daniel glances across and sees me watching. He grins. 'What?'

'That was so cool.'

He looks embarrassed. 'I just talk to him like I talk to my little sister, Sam, when she's kicking off.' He pats Onyx and looks out across the landscape: gently sloping hills in varying shades of green and brown, a river winding its way through trees, a speckling of houses and villages, and some grey roads snaking alongside the fields. 'This is pretty good, isn't it?'

'I can't believe we're so close to Ryton Stoke and yet we're basically in the countryside,' I marvel, reaching into the bag at my waist to pull out my phone.

'You brought your phone?' Daniel laughs and shakes his head. 'You're addicted.'

'I am not! But our fans want to know what we're up to!' I tell him, trying to video the panorama without dropping either the phone or one of my whips.

'Our fans.' Daniel is properly chuckling now.

'Don't sneer,' I tell him sternly. 'We have over four thousand followers, you know.'

'Four *thousand*?!' His eyes widen.

'Not laughing now, are you?'

'You should put that away.' Tanya has ridden up beside me. Silver is snorting and tossing his head and trying to reach the grass. Tanya keeps yanking on the reins, which I'm sure can't be kind on Silver's mouth.

I scowl at her. 'Don't tell me what to do.'

'It's not safe to use your phone while riding,' says Tanya sanctimoniously. 'It's a safety hazard.'

'So you're an instructor now, are you?' I snap.

'Ellie!' Fee calls from the back of the group. 'Put that phone away, please!'

Tanya grins at me maliciously. 'Told you.' Silver stops dead and reaches down determinedly to take a mouthful of grass, and Tanya is nearly pulled over his head. I snort with laughter while I stuff my phone back in my pocket.

Rumana gets us to stop together and then suggests some trotting for those who feel comfortable. Jessie squirms and says she's not sure, and I feel really bad for her. This is the girl who used to jump 90 cm without even blinking! 'You don't have to,' Rumana tells her kindly. 'It's entirely up to you.'

Eventually Jessie says she'll try, and so the whole ten of us move into a trot across the grassland. I still don't remember everyone's name, but I think there's Finn and Luke (the boys sharing a room with Daniel), and an Annabel – and one other girl. 'What's that girl called?' I ask Summer, who has trotted Luna up next to me. I point to the one I mean. 'In the green hat silk, on the palomino.'

'Kizzy,' says Summer. 'She's nice; she's in the bedroom next to me and Jessie.' She giggles. 'She raced into our room last night at about eleven o'clock because she saw a spider. I had to go and get it out of her room. It was teeny! But both she and Skye are really scared of spiders. Kizzy gave me a whole pack of rainbow laces as a thank you, and Jessie and me scoffed the lot in the middle of the night!'

I feel a sharp pang of jealousy. I wish I were sharing a bedroom upstairs with all the others.

Rumana brings us to a halt again and asks for a show of hands for those who would like to canter. To my surprise, Jessie puts her hand up. Of course I put mine up too! So do Daniel and Finn and Tanya. The others shake their heads nervously. 'Right,' says Rumana. 'Those of you who are going to canter – you're with me. Fee, you're in charge of the rest – but I'd like your group to stick with walking, all right?'

Fee nods.

'Can you all see that gate right at the far end of this field?' asks Rumana. In a gap in a row of trees there's a small, barred gate. 'We'll all meet up there, OK? And then we'll head back single file along the lane.' Her own horse suddenly tries to take a nip at Molly's Echo, who's standing nearby. 'No, thank you,' says Rumana sternly, and turns him in a circle. 'Right. The cantering party with me, please. The ground is mostly firm, but sudden dips can catch you out. Stay very steady in the saddle, strong core – here we go!'

She kicks her horse into action, and the rest of us take off after her. Elvis moves quickly from an extended trot into a canter, and it feels like we're *flying* along! I've never cantered outside of the arena, and it feels completely different: the blue of the sky, the wind on my face, the thud of the hooves – it makes me shout in pure joy! To my right I hear an answering whoop as Daniel canters on Onyx, his face as delighted as mine. I glance to my left and see Jessie, her face set and focused, her body poised just above the saddle like a jockey. She looks so professional! I'm not convinced she's actually enjoying it, but she's not having a panic attack, so that's good. Tanya is bouncing around as ever, completely ignoring what Rumana just said about staying steady, and I feel sorry for poor Silver.

I LOVE riding. I mean, I know I've said it before, but this – this is just the best feeling in the entire world. My mum once went on this retreat where they talked about the connectedness of everything. Did you know everything is made from stardust? Everything in our world: trees, plastic, stone, bone, brain, trains, musical instruments, teachers, water, seaweed, fire – everything you can touch is made

from the same stuff. We're basically all connected to everything.

To be fair, I thought Mum was talking a lot of waffle at first, but there's something about opening yourself up to the wide world, breathing it in – you can just *feel* that you're a tiny part of a huge, important whole. I believe it, right through to my heart, my soul. I only get this feeling when I'm riding. The wind, the horse, the world around me: *we're all connected*.

Well, that is until Finn's horse spooks at a rock sticking out of the ground and disconnects Finn from his saddle!

Rumana spots it, and waves to the rest of us. I slow Elvis and take him back round to where Rumana has caught up with Finn, who is sitting on the ground looking decidedly cross. She slides off and crouches down next to him. I can't hear what they're saying, but Finn soon gets up, brushes dirt off his breeches and gets back up on his pony thanks to a leg-up from Rumana.

'Well done, everyone, for stopping,' says Rumana,

smiling at us all. 'Some lovely cantering going on. We'll walk the rest of the way and then have a rest at the gate, OK?' She vaults easily back on to her own horse, and we walk sedately the hundred metres or so to the gate.

'You OK?' I hear Daniel ask Jessie.

Jessie takes a deep breath. 'Yeah. Yeah, I think I am. That was kind of intense.' She laughs. 'But I did it, and I feel OK. For the moment, anyway.'

'That's brilliant!'

'Yes,' I add. 'That's amazing, Jessie. You'll be competing again in no time.'

Her face looks doubtful. 'Oh, I don't know about that.'

'One step at a time,' agrees Daniel. He smiles at her.

I feel a bit grouchy suddenly, but it's probably because I'm hungry again.

The rest of the hack takes us mostly along narrow footpaths between hedges, and I find myself longing to be cantering across the open grassland again. Some of the ponies are a bit too fond of stopping to take bites out of hedges and grass on our way, and of course every time one of them does a wee, we all have to stop and wait! Rumana's horse *definitely* doesn't like Echo, so Molly moves further down the line. I hear Tanya telling her she needs to relax in the saddle more and Molly murmuring something in response.

The only time there's a real problem is when we meet a couple with a dog coming the other way. They stop and wait for us to come past, and the dog won't stop barking. I can tell some of the horses don't like the noise. Elvis's ears go right back, so I try to channel Daniel's calm horse whispering and talk to Elvis in a low steady voice as we pass the dog. You'd have thought the couple might look apologetic about their noisy dog, but they seem more annoyed with the line of horses!

'Well done, everyone,' says Rumana as we arrive back at Berry Farm. 'Some fantastic riding this afternoon! Finn, well done for getting straight back into the saddle – you can have a team point for that. And, Ellie – I'm really impressed with your control and connection with Elvis, so a team point for you too. Well done!'

I GLOW with pride. I mean, it's not about the winning, I know (except, it's VERY cool to be contributing to my team), but just getting a point because I'm a good rider – I feel very proud.

'Well done, Ellie,' says Molly, smiling at me. 'I'm really pleased for you.'

'Aww, thanks.'

'Hopefully I can get a team point soon too,' she says.

'I'm sure you will!' I tell her.

'Oh, I don't know. The rest of you are all so good. I know I need to relax a bit more. And take control. I'm just not very good at those things. I'm always being told that at home.' She laughs but it's a little too forced, and I feel like the shine has suddenly faded from my achievement. Why is Molly so down on herself all the time?

# Chapter 10

Back at the stables, we rub down the ponies, and the yard girls come to check on all our tack. Hacking out in the open means even more opportunities to get saddles and bridles dirty, and grass seeds and burrs can get stuck under saddle pads. Pretty much everyone has some cleaning to do! In all the chaos of saddle soap and sponges and water buckets, I hear Finn, Luke and Henry complaining they can't find their kits. 'I'm coming round in five minutes and will be awarding team points to the cleanest tack I can find!' calls Fee, and there's a howl of outrage from Henry.

'Someone's nicked it! I swear! It was right here!' The three boys are standing together outside Henry's stable, looking annoyed. Their yellow ribbons flutter in the breeze, and I frown. All three from the same team? All three with missing kits? That's three possible points the yellow team can't win – isn't that a bit of a coincidence?

I mention it to Summer, who shrugs and says, 'Maybe they're just a bit forgetful? The boys in my class are always losing things.'

'Hey,' says Daniel, coming past with a bowl of soapy water. 'Some boys are very organized, thanks very much!'

'Not the ones in my class,' says Summer, shaking her head.

'Don't you think it's strange they're all in the same team, though?' I persist.

'Not really. Have you finished? Fee's heading over.'

Fee checks over our tack and proclaims it clean enough that we can stop. Summer gets a team point for being super-clean while Fee finds a bit of grass still stuck in Elvis's bit, so I remain point-less. I don't really mind though, because I'm more interested in why the yellow team has been targeted. Has someone got a grudge against them? Quickly, I jot down the facts in my Case Notes book. Ideally, I'd like to interview the three boys, but there isn't time.

'Come and gather over here!' Hattie is calling. We all hurry over to the grassy area outside the accommodation block.

Once everyone is sitting down, Tobi explains about the Musical Ride. 'On Saturday morning when your parents come to collect you, we'll do a performance,' she starts, and my heart leaps. I LOVE performing! I think I get it from my mum. 'We want you to get into your two groups – Oscar's and Rumana's – and pick a song or piece of music that you'd like to use. Then over the next few days, you'll come up with the choreography and have rehearsals. All ten of you have to be in the arena on horseback at the same time. You can do circles, diagonals, walking, trotting, crossovers – whatever you can think of that fits with the music. You can even use props, as long as they're not too complicated and you check with us first. You've got the next hour to decide on your music and to start planning your choreography.'

You won't BELIEVE how hard it is to choose a song. Jessie wants Harry Styles, and I want Taylor Swift, and NO ONE can agree. Tanya wastes everyone's time talking about seeing *The Lion King* in London. In the end we only make a decision because Tobi gets cross and says we're out of time. It comes down to a vote between 'The Greatest Show' and 'Defying Gravity', which are both from musicals that I don't know. 'Defying Gravity' just wins out, but then we discover Oscar's group has picked 'We're All in This Together' from *High School Musical*, which is SO MUCH BETTER.

I try to interview Henry at dinner about the missing kit, but he stares at me like I'm loopy and takes his tray to the other end of the canteen.

'It's not a mystery, Ellie,' says Jessie as we scoff down lasagne and garlic bread. 'They just lost their stuff. People do.'

I frown at my plate. 'But they're all in the same team.'

'Coincidence.'

'Huh.'

'Team points total!' calls Geraldine, and we all sit up, suddenly silent. 'The green team is trailing on fourteen – don't worry, lots of opportunities to make that up tomorrow! The yellow team took an early lead but has stalled on sixteen. The purple and red teams are sitting on seventeen points each. And the blue team is pulling ahead on nineteen!'

'YESSS!' I punch the air and beam at my friends. Out of the corner of my eye, I can see Tanya scowling, which makes me even happier. The four of us high-five each other.

'Now, eat up and clear away quickly,' says Geraldine, 'because we've got a surprise for everyone in the arena. Meet outside in twenty minutes; you won't want to miss this!'

As she sits down, everyone erupts into excited discussion. 'Nineteen points!' says Summer. 'That's amazing!'

'What do you think the surprise is?' asks Daniel.

'A unicorn!' I say, and everyone laughs.

Jessie takes a sharp breath in. 'What if – what if it's Samira Kennedy?'

Samira Kennedy is Jessie's idol and came to give out the trophies at Starlight's summer show. She is *very* cool.

'No way,' says Summer. 'It couldn't be – could it?'

It isn't. Everyone's sitting on blankets on the ground outside the arena (well, except me – I'm in my chair), passing sweets around, and there's a bunch of five girls aged maybe nine to fifteen dressed in matching blue catsuits in the arena, two women, and a black horse.

'We're thrilled,' says Geraldine in a loud voice, 'to welcome the junior vaulting team from Ryton Stoke. They're going to start off by showing us a display of what they can do, and then

they're going to talk us through the basics of vaulting.'

'I thought vaulting was gymnastics?' Summer whispers to me. 'You know, like the vaulting horse we have at school – *oh*!' Her eyes widen. 'Is that why it's called a horse?!'

I don't have time to reply because music is starting up, and one of the women stands in the middle of the arena holding a long lunge line attached to the black horse's bridle. She encourages the horse into a trot and then a slow canter, sending it round and round in a big circle. She holds the longest thinnest whip I've ever seen just behind it – I guess to make sure he keeps going? The other woman stays by the edge of the arena.

We all fall silent as one of the girls runs alongside the horse, sticks an arm up in the air, grabs one of the handles attached to the saddle – actually, is it a saddle? No, it looks more like a kind of leather roll on top of a large saddle pad – and swings herself up backwards! My jaw drops. The girl gets to her feet and stands on the back of the horse, arms wide, as it canters round and round. Then she leans forward to grasp the handles again and swings one leg up into an arabesque!

'How is she *doing* that?' I hear Daniel exclaim. 'That's incredible!'

It gets more and more impressive. Another girl joins the first, and supports her in a handstand – a *handstand*, on the back of a cantering horse! – and then the two of them go through a sequence of movements and poses with hardly a wobble. They jump down and are replaced by a second pair who do equally impressive poses and balances – and then one of them gets on the other's shoulders! And a THIRD joins them!

None of us can take our eyes off the display; it's absolutely amazing. When they finally finish, and the horse comes to a halt, we burst into applause. The five girls come and stand in a line and take a bow, grinning at each other.

The woman who had been standing by the edge comes to the front now and introduces herself as Emily. 'Thank you very much,' she says. 'Now, I know all of you are riders, and maybe some of you do gymnastics as well. But have you ever thought of combining the two?'

The vaulting team brings over a large barrel, and Emily talks us through the exercises they do. They even invite Skye, from our camp, to have a go at an arabesque!

Then Emily calls over the other woman and the horse, whose name is Bertie. 'Bertie is wearing some very special tack, as you'll have seen,' she says. 'This piece here, with the handles, is the roller, and it's the most important part of the equipment – it has to be comfortable for the horse, and it has to be completely secure – if you grab it and it slips sideways, you could have a nasty accident!'

The girls then show us the barrel positions on Bertie as he canters around again on the lunge line. By the time the display is over, we're all MASSIVELY impressed and I clap until my hands are sore. As everyone gets up, Daniel says, 'Wish I could have a go. I reckon I could do that.'

I turn to him, scoffing, 'No way. You're kidding, right?'

Instead of replying, Daniel suddenly tips forward into a handstand and walks seven paces on his hands!

'WHAAAAT!' I scream, and everyone around me starts exclaiming. 'I didn't know you could do that! That's incredible!'

Daniel turns the right way up again, wiping his hands on his trousers and grinning. 'Yeah, well, you don't know *everything* about me.'

'What else don't we know?' I challenge him.

He laughs. 'I guess you'll just have to wait to find out.'

# Chapter 11

'Yeah, I got three extra team points,' I hear Tanya saying loudly as I come into the canteen the next morning. 'I groomed Fee's pony for her before he went into the stable for the night. She said she'd give me a point – but there are *three* more there this morning; I guess she felt generous!'

'Did you hear that?' I say to my friends as we sit down. 'Tanya earned three extra team points for grooming Fee's pony! That takes the red team into the lead!'

'*Three?*' exclaims Jessie. 'That's a bit much!'

'Do you think we should offer to do extra chores?' Summer asks anxiously.

'We could, I suppose.' I glance over to the yard girls' table, where Tanya has sat down next to Fee and is chatting and laughing with her. 'I dunno. I didn't come to pony camp to do other people's work for them.'

'Me neither,' says Daniel with feeling. 'I do enough chores in real life!'

'Is everything OK at home?' I ask.

He makes an 'eek' kind of face. 'I think Aunt Jo is a bit stressed. Alfie sends me angry texts saying he's not allowed to do anything. He's mad that I'm away. I think he's just mad at everything at the moment.'

'Oh, I'm sorry.'

He gives me a smile. 'Thanks for asking, Ellie. I try not to think about it too much. It's nice to have a break – and to hang out with the coolest people I know.'

On our way out of the canteen I check the score chart and see that the red team has three more stickers than it did last night, taking it into first place just one point ahead of our blue team. I'm a bit surprised that Fee added the stickers herself instead of waiting for them to be added to Geraldine's score sheet today, but maybe Geraldine said it was OK.

Our morning is spent doing an introduction to cross-country (AMAZING!! Though Jessie decides not to ride because she feels wobbly) and stable management with Geraldine, who divides us into teams and grills us on the different pieces of tack, the rules of feeding, how to select the right length of stirrups, and all kinds of other things. 'Excellent work,' she says, looking pleased. 'Blue team, are you? Well, I think you're the most knowledgeable group I've had so far. Take a point each. I'll add them to my tally today.'

'That's four more points for our team!' I say, exultant, as we head to lunch. 'Take that, Tanya!'

We're all sitting at our table eating rolls and crisps when Geraldine comes into the canteen carrying a bunch of pretty pink flowers tied with a red ribbon. 'Who left this beautiful bunch of flowers on my desk?' she calls to everyone.

We look at each other and around the room. Everyone is shrugging and shaking their heads.

'Someone must have,' she says. 'Well, whoever it is, thank you. It's a very kind gesture, and I appreciate it.'

She's about to go when Fee speaks up. 'It's tied with a red ribbon, like the ones we gave out to the teams.'

'It *is*.' Geraldine becomes thoughtful. 'Is anyone in the red team missing their ribbon?'

Molly and two other members of the red team hold out their own ribbons.

'Oh,' says Tanya. 'I don't know where mine is.'

I frown.

'Could this be yours, Tanya?' asks Geraldine, untying the ribbon from the flowers.

Tanya goes over to have a look at it. 'Well, it *could* be,' she says, 'but I don't know *how* it got to be on that beautiful bunch of flowers . . . I mean, I *definitely* don't know anything about it.' She blinks several times at Geraldine.

My jaw drops. I can see exactly what she's doing!

Geraldine smiles down at Tanya. 'Well, perhaps since it's your ribbon on the flowers, I should assume they were from you.'

Tanya does the worst bit of play-acting I've ever seen – and I've sat through all the performances of my mum's amateur theatre group! She giggles and shuffles her feet and behaves as though she's some kind of toddler asking for praise.

And Geraldine falls for it! 'Take a team point,' she says, patting Tanya on the head.

'No!' I breathe, as Tanya goes back to her table looking infuriatingly smug.

Daniel gives a half-admiring laugh. 'That was quite a performance.'

'Exactly what I was thinking!' I exclaim.

'What do you mean?' asks Summer.

'That!' I wave my arm. 'What she just did. Pretending she'd given Geraldine the flowers.'

Summer looks puzzled. 'Did she not then?'

'She didn't *say* she did,' says Jessie.

'Oh, I'm confused now,' says Summer. 'They were tied with her ribbon, weren't they?'

'They were tied with *a* ribbon,' I say. 'Tanya can't prove it was hers.'

Molly gets up. 'I've finished – catch you at the stables in a minute.' She takes her leftover roll with her and dumps it in the bin on her way out.

'What are you trying to say, Ellie?' asks Jessie.

'I don't know! Daniel – you saw it, right?'

He nods. 'Well – I saw someone taking an opportunity.'

I'm disgusted. 'It's just sucking up to Geraldine.'

'Oh,' says Summer. 'I was just thinking it would be a nice thing to do. Geraldine must have a lot of work to do organizing this.'

I make a noise of frustration. 'Doesn't it bother you all how much of a pain Tanya is?'

The others exchange surprised looks. 'Um,' says Jessie. 'I hadn't really noticed.'

'She wasn't the one who mentioned the red ribbon, though,' Daniel points out. 'That was Fee.'

'Maybe they're in it together!' I say dramatically. 'Fee gave Tanya THREE points for grooming her horse, remember!'

He laughs and shakes his head. 'I think you're seeing a conspiracy where there isn't one.'

'It's all those mystery stories she reads,' says Jessie, and the others chuckle.

I'm indignant. 'I can't believe you guys haven't noticed what's going on. It's right under your noses!'

Jessie shrugs. 'If Tanya wants to try and earn extra team points, I don't see there's anything wrong with that. We could do it too.'

Daniel sees me about to interrupt, and jumps in. 'El, it's not worth getting worked up over.'

I quite like being called El. Daniel's never called me El before. 'Huh,' I say, mollified. 'Maybe.'

When the others start a new conversation, Daniel leans over and whispers, 'I know you're itching to start a new Case File.'

'Shurrup.'

He laughs.

Case #25: The Mysterious Appearing Bunch of Flowers

Location: Geraldine's office

Date: Thurs 26th October

Time: 12.56 p.m.

Description: Someone left a bunch of pink flowers tied with a red ribbon on Geraldine's desk. Fee pointed out the red ribbon. Tanya said her own ribbon was missing. She didn't actually SAY she'd given Geraldine the flowers, but she didn't say she DIDN'T. Geraldine gave the red team a point!!!

Prime Suspects: Tanya and Fee.

Fee was the one who pointed out the red ribbon. Tanya said hers was missing. IS IT REALLY? She might have hidden it when Geraldine asked the red team to show their ribbons.

If the ribbon is still in Tanya's pocket, it would mean she definitely DIDN'T give Geraldine the flowers and has benefited ILLEGALLY.

Plan of Action: check Tanya's pockets?? How??

# Chapter 12

Even though I'd rather talk to anyone else, I deliberately propel myself up to Tanya as we set off back to the stables after lunch. 'Hey, Tanya,' I say.

She glances at me sideways. 'What do you want?'

'Wow, that's a bit rude,' I say, then try to make my voice sound friendly. 'I just came over to say that was a nice thing you did for Geraldine, getting her flowers like that.'

'Oh, right.' She speeds up a bit, trying to get ahead of me. I increase my speed too.

'Have you got a tissue or anything?' I ask, pretending to sneeze. 'I've got a runny nose.'

She starts to reach for her pocket, and then her hand seems to hesitate. 'No,' she says, dropping her hand back to her side. 'Sorry.'

VERY suspicious! What if the missing ribbon is in her pocket and she's afraid I might see it? I'd investigate further, but we have to get ready for mounted games, which are like party games on ponies. Have you ever taken part in an egg-and-spoon race? Or an obstacle course? Mounted games are like that, only on a horse. Balancing a beanbag on your head while you weave between poles, or carrying a plastic cup on the end of a stick from one end of the arena to the other. It can get very exciting and loud and silly, and everyone is keen to get started.

Even Jessie is back on Angus after her wobble this morning. Mounted games don't involve any jumping, so it's suitable for almost any ability.

We're all tacked up and Tobi has lifted me up into

the saddle, but there's nothing set up in the arena, just Rumana talking urgently to Geraldine. When they see us approaching, Rumana calls out, 'Hi everyone. Sorry about this, got a bit of an issue. All the games equipment has gone – I don't know how. Or where. But it's just – missing. The whole lot.'

We all stare at each other while Geraldine and Rumana try to figure out what to do. Then some of our group tie up their ponies and go looking. I wish I could help but I'm stuck up on Elvis, and he's suddenly decided that one of the fence posts is delicious, so I'm fully occupied trying to get him to stop chewing it. What I REALLY want to be doing is writing up yet another curious case in my Case Notes book. Pony camp is turning out to be full of mysteries, and I feel like I haven't solved ANY of them yet!

After fifteen minutes, there's a sudden whiff of excitement and Geraldine and Rumana come back into the arena, holding aloft two enormous boxes packed with the missing equipment. Molly, looking decidedly rosy in the face, comes to untie Echo. 'Where was it?' I ask her.

'I found it right at the back of the bales of shavings,' she says. 'So weird.'

'Fantastic searching, everyone!' calls Geraldine as Rumana hastily sets up a game. 'And Molly – a team point for your eagle eyes.'

Molly almost dissolves with pride and I beam at her. 'Well done,' I say. 'What made you look there?'

She shrugs. 'Fee sent us all off in different directions. And I wouldn't have checked behind the bales at all if I hadn't seen a flag sticking up. Just luck, I guess.'

'Nice work, Molly,' says Tanya, and Molly flushes with pleasure.

'Thanks, Tanya.'

The mounted games are a lot of fun after that, but I find it hard to concentrate properly. Why would anyone hide the equipment? It would have been found eventually anyway, and all it did was delay our session and make Rumana and Geraldine annoyed. It seems completely pointless.

Except it wasn't *completely* pointless, because Molly won a point for her team and that made her happy. So that's nice. Another point for the red team . . .

*Wait.*

'Ellie, what are you doing?' My teammates are yelling at me and I realize I've gone round the cone in the wrong direction.

'Oops, sorry!' I turn Elvis, but we've lost precious seconds. I have to focus after that, but when the game is over and Rumana is setting up a new one, I take the opportunity to whisper to Molly, 'You know earlier, when you were searching? Can you tell me exactly what happened?'

She looks puzzled. 'Why?'

'Oh, you know me and my mysteries,' I say airily. 'Can't help myself.'

She laughs. 'You're so funny. Well, so ... um ... let me think. Hattie and Fee were in the yard, sweeping. A bunch of us started looking in stables and stuff, and Fee got annoyed, asking us what we were doing. So we explained, and Hattie said we would cover more ground if we did it systematically. Like, if each person looked in a different area? And Fee basically took over and started ordering us around, telling us who should look where.' She frowns, trying to remember what happened next. 'Fee told me to check the feed room, but Hattie said someone else was already near there ... So then Fee said Tanya and I should check the storage room round the other side, where the shavings are. And Hattie said good idea – so that's where we went. And then I found the equipment.'

I'm nodding and nodding, my brain whirring along at a hundred miles an hour. 'So it was *Fee* who told you to check the storage room. You *and* Tanya.'

'Well, yeah. Why?'

'Oh, nothing.'

But it's not nothing. Fee deliberately sent Tanya and Molly off to the place where the equipment was hidden. What if *Tanya* was meant to find it, not Molly? Since they're both in the same team, I guess it doesn't matter which of them did the actual finding.

Yet again, Fee is indirectly responsible for the red team getting another point. Is she doing it on purpose? But why?

My brain whirrs and whirrs during the rest of the mounted games. I can't stop wondering about Fee. She gave Tanya three points for grooming her pony. She told Tanya where to look for the equipment. Surely it can't be a coincidence? Why would she be helping Tanya to win points?

There are lots of reasons why you might help someone else to win. You might be good friends with them. (Maybe Tanya and Fee know each other from way back?) You might want someone else to *lose*. (Does Fee have a grudge against someone else here?) Or it might be because they're *making* you help them. What if Tanya is *blackmailing* Fee somehow? Maybe Tanya knows a secret about Fee and is threatening to tell?

I have to find out more.

When the mounted games are finished, we give the ponies a break. There's still plenty to do around the yard, though. 'I've never seen so much poo,' moans Summer, scooping up yet another pile and dumping it in a wheelbarrow.

'I have,' says Daniel. 'At the Starlight summer show day. Remember I was on poo duty in the outdoor school? I don't know how many barrows of poo I shovelled that day. My arms were killing me by the end of it.'

'Good thing you have such strong arms,' I say, and Jessie and Summer burst into giggles. I look at them crossly. 'What?'

'Nothing, nothing,' says Jessie.

Molly calls to us from the end of the yard, 'Guys! There's some lemonade here!'

'Any biscuits?' I call back.

'Yes, loads. Some Jammie Dodgers, I think.'

'I'm there!' exclaims Summer, making us all laugh. I think Summer would live on Jammie Dodgers if she could!

As I arrive at the picnic area, I keep a sharp lookout for Fee and Tanya. To my delight, they're both here – chatting together at the far end of one of the picnic benches. I stare across at them, my eyes narrowed. They look cheerful enough. But maybe it's all an act? What if Tanya is instructing Fee in the next part of her devilish plan? I won't know unless I can get close enough to hear what they're saying. I drop a couple of biscuits in my lap and grab a lemonade.

'Would you like me to carry that for you?' offers Molly.

'No, I'm good.'

Carefully, I manoeuvre myself around the outside of the group, trying to look natural. Tanya and Fee are deep in conversation. If I can just get a bit closer –

'Here you go, Ellie.' Someone grabs the handles of my chair and pushes me briskly over to the nearest bench where three girls are sitting and chatting.

'No thanks, I –'

'Oh, that's OK.' Geraldine beams down at me. 'Everything all right? How was mounted games in the end?'

'Oh – great, yeah.' I'm really cross. Not only did she grab my handles without asking, but she's wheeled me over to a group of girls I don't actually know, and right in the opposite direction from Fee and Tanya!

'I'm so glad you're here,' Geraldine goes on. 'I've thought for some time that it would be great if we could make our events more inclusive. It's so important that people like you get access to the same opportunities as everyone else.'

*People like me?*

'And it's great for the other children to see that a disability doesn't have to hold you back. You're just the same as them when you're on a horse. You can achieve fantastic things.' She beams. 'You're such an inspiration, Ellie. The instructors and the yard girls and the mums have all said what a cheerful, happy presence you are. They're so impressed with how you handle everything.'

There's a buzzing noise, and she pulls out her phone, still smiling at me. 'Sorry, I've got to take this. Keep up the good work!' She heads off, swiping the screen and saying, 'Hello? Thanks for getting back to me. I wanted to check on . . .'

The three other girls at the table look at me curiously. 'You OK?' one of them asks.

'Fine,' I say through gritted teeth.

'She's really nice, isn't she?' the girl adds. 'Geraldine, I mean.'

'Yeah. Sorry. I have to . . . be somewhere else.'

I leave my lemonade and my biscuits on the table and move away from the crowd. I've lost my appetite.

Daniel comes to find me a few minutes later. I'm staring at the stone wall of the building, wishing I could kick it. 'You OK?'

'Yeah, fine, whatever.'

'Hey, what's happened?' He slides down the

160

wall and sits on the ground, looking up at me. It makes a change. Usually, everyone looks down on me.

'Nothing. It's fine. Geraldine said . . .' I trail off. 'It doesn't matter.'

'Well, it obviously *does* matter,' says Daniel. 'I'm an expert on grumpy people, remember? I have four brothers and a sister.'

'I'm not grumpy, I'm angry. You wouldn't understand.'

'Ellie, you *know* I understand anger!'

'Huh. I guess. It's just – I don't know how to say it.' I look down at my hands. I feel like a deflating balloon. 'It's hard to explain. Geraldine said some stuff to me. She thought she was being nice. But the words she used . . .'

'What words?'

'She said it was great to see people like me taking part in things with everyone else.'

Daniel's eyebrows crease in the middle. 'People like you? What does that mean?'

'Disabled people,' I say. 'Wheelchair users.'

'Ohhh. Oh, right.' His frown deepens. 'What a weird thing to say.'

'Not really. People say that kind of thing all the time. And she said I was an inspiration. All the grown-ups were impressed with me for being happy.'

Now his eyebrows seem to climb up his forehead. 'For being happy?! Does she think you should be crying all the time? What, cos you hurt your back?'

I let out a snort. 'Yeah, probably. I think they think I'm some kind of, I dunno – a little soldier. I suppose I should be grateful she didn't say I was *brave*.'

Daniel looks puzzled. 'Brave for what?'

'Who knows! People say it all the time.'

He shakes his head. 'Well, it sounds like she said it all wrong, even if she was trying to be nice. I'm sorry.'

'Thank you.' I nod. 'That's it. And now I feel rubbish.'

He thinks for a moment and then says, 'I have something that'll make you feel better.'

'What?'

Daniel digs into his pocket and pulls out a rather squished chocolate mini roll, still in its purple wrapper. 'This. It might not look like much, but it's actually magic.'

I try not to smile. 'Magic?' I echo sarcastically.

'I'm not kidding. It may look like an ordinary mini roll, but it's not. I bought this one from a mysterious shopkeeper in a shop that *isn't there any more.*' He looks at me very seriously. 'This shopkeeper told me that whoever ate this mini roll would have the power to rise above all hurtful things. That it would give them invisible armour. Anything anyone said or did to them after that would bounce off, like arrows off a shield. Now, I can see you're suspicious – I was too! No way, I said, you're having me on. "Trust me," he said. "This mini roll is magic." So I bought it and I put it in my pocket, and the next time I walked down that street, the shop had gone.'

I'm properly laughing now. 'You're such an idiot.'

'I've kept it in my pocket for exactly the right moment,' he says, still not cracking a smile. 'But I think you need it more than me, so I am gifting it to you.' He holds it out, his hands flat, his head bowed. 'Here. Take the magic mini roll and don your invisible armour.'

'Daniel.' I roll my eyes.

'Oh well, if you don't *want* the magic mini –' He goes to put it back in his pocket, but I snatch it from his hands.

'No, I'll have it, it's good.' I tear open the wrapper and start eating it. He grins at me. 'I didn't know you could make up stories.'

'Like I said, you don't know everything about me.' He gets to his feet, brushing himself down. 'Looks like people are moving off. It's the Musical Ride rehearsal next – you coming?'

'Yeah. I'll just finish putting on my armour.'

He nods. 'See you there.'

I know the mini roll isn't magic – I *know* that – but somehow, as I lick the last bit of chocolate off the wrapper, I do feel a bit stronger.

# Chapter 13

The Musical Ride rehearsal is pretty much a disaster – have you ever tried getting ten different people to plan something together and then practise it? It doesn't help that one of those people is Tanya, who's determined to choreograph the whole thing herself and not let any of the rest of us have a turn. 'I've done this loads of times before,' she keeps saying.

'Twice,' says one of the others. 'You said you'd done pony camp *twice* before.'

'Yes, well, that's two more than most of you, isn't it?' says Tanya. 'So it makes sense if I'm in charge.'

'This is supposed to be a *team* effort,' says Jessie.

'Yeah, you're not the boss,' I add.

Tanya's face goes red. 'I'm just *saying* I know how to do this.'

'How about we all get a chance to suggest a move?' says Daniel, in his peacemaking voice. 'And then maybe you could work out how to string them together, Tanya?'

Tanya grudgingly accepts this idea, but then complains that everyone else's suggestions are rubbish. By the end of our session time, we haven't got much further than working out the first two moves.

'I've never felt more glad to get back to mucking out,' says Daniel when we arrive at the yard. 'Give me poo over a musical rehearsal any day!'

'You OK, Molly?' asks Hattie, as Molly leads Echo past me and ties him up at the stable.

Molly shrugs. 'I'm OK.'

She looks a bit upset, if I'm honest, and I remember that she doesn't like confrontation, but before I can offer any support, Tobi arrives to lift me down into my chair. By the time I've got myself sorted, Molly is deep in conversation with Hattie, who is making consoling noises.

It feels like we've already had an action-packed afternoon, but it turns out there's a voluntary activity planned for the hour before dinner: archery! Geraldine calls everyone together and says we can choose whether to take part in a short archery lesson or whether we'd like to spend the time chilling out. 'Have a quick think,' she says to us all, 'and I'll ask for a show of hands in two minutes.'

'I really want a sit-down,' says Summer. 'I'm so tired already!'

'Me too,' says Jessie. 'After all that arguing, ugh!'

Molly says hesitantly, 'We could go and flop on those comfy chairs in the big lounge?'

'Yes! I want to go on my phone for a bit,' says Jessie.

Daniel nods. 'Sounds good. I mean, archery is cool and everything, but I'm knackered – and we've got karaoke this evening after dinner, haven't we?'

'So we'll all say no to archery then?' says Jessie, looking round at us.

We nod back. 'I could do some social media posts,' I say. 'I've got a bit behind.'

But when Geraldine calls for a show of hands to see who's interested in the archery, Tanya puts up her hand. My eyes swivel to Fee, who's standing with the archery instructor, holding a quiver of arrows.

Before I know it, I've put up my hand too. The others stare at me.

'What are you doing, Ellie?' asks Jessie. 'I thought you were going to come to the lounge with us?'

'I've got an idea,' I whisper. 'I think maybe Tanya is getting Fee to help her win points. Maybe she has some kind of hold over her. Like a secret.'

'What?' says Jessie blankly. 'What on earth are you talking about?'

'A secret?' says Summer. 'What do you mean?'

'Remember when the boys lost their cleaning kits?' I say. 'I bet Fee hid them all. Tanya couldn't because she was in a lesson, but Fee had access. They're working together – and I think Tanya is the mastermind.'

Jessie and Summer catch each other's eye and both start laughing. 'OK, Detective Pikachu,' says Jessie, shaking her head as she giggles. 'Whatever you say.'

I glare at her. 'It's not funny.'

'I love your imagination, Ellie,' says Summer, smiling at me fondly, which only makes me crosser.

'I wish I hadn't told you all now,' I snap.

'Oh, don't be upset,' says Molly, looking anxious. 'It's only that . . . well, it seems . . . I dunno – unlikely.'

'Unlikely doesn't mean impossible,' I say, exasperated. 'That's why I have to investigate – to find the evidence. It's fine, none of you have to come.'

Geraldine calls for the archery group to leave, so I follow them out of the canteen and off to a field on the other side of the arena, far from any horses

169

or people who could get in the way of accidental arrows.

To my intense annoyance, I have to ask for help when we get to the field – the grass is just a bit too long to be able to push myself easily. But it's Fee who comes to push, so it gives me an opportunity to start up a conversation.

'Thanks,' I say. 'I hate asking for help but sometimes you just have to, don't you?'

'That's true,' agrees Fee.

'And it's nice to help others,' I press on as we bump over the grass. I clutch the sides of my chair to stabilize myself. 'Don't you think?'

'Yeah.' I can't see her face, but Fee sounds like she's not properly paying attention.

I decide to try something more direct. 'Though sometimes people make us help, don't they? I had a friend once who said I had to do her maths homework for her or she'd tell everyone I fancied this boy. So I did. Has anything like that ever happened to you?'

'Er . . .' Fee sounds a bit confused. 'I'm not sure what you – oh, here we are.'

We have reached the rest of the group and I burst out in a final attempt, 'You know you should tell someone if you're being threatened, right?'

Fee stares at me in what looks like complete astonishment.

'Ellie,' says Nina, the mum who helps out in the accommodation block. She's wearing some kind of arm strap and holding a bow. 'You ready to listen?'

'Yeah – yes,' I say, feeling a jolt of uncertainty. Fee didn't respond like someone who was being blackmailed. Maybe she's helping Tanya for another reason?

It turns out that Nina is an archery instructor. She talks us through all the safety advice and then shows us how to stand or sit facing sideways on from the target, how to stretch your arm out straight and then pull back the string. Before long, we're all having a go with the five bows she's brought for us to try.

'This is *very* cool,' I say, as I finally manage to get my arrow into the outer part of the target.

Nina grins at me. 'You're doing great, Ellie.'

I'm doing better than Tanya, which is extremely

satisfying. She keeps making a huffing noise every time she misses, and then saying loudly that there must be something wrong with her bow. Nina takes it from her and checks it over before handing it back, saying, 'It's tuned correctly. Perhaps try taking your time over the aiming moment – don't rush.'

Tanya sees me watching her and says in a snarky tone, 'Something on your mind, Ellie?'

I make a rude face in response.

Fee and Tobi get very good, very quickly. 'Shame you yard girls can't earn team points!' Nina says approvingly as Tobi hits a bullseye.

Nina splits us into two teams and we have a bit of a tournament, which is pretty fun. Tanya and Fee are both in my team, and while I had thought I'd try to get Tanya to talk, I'm finding it harder and harder just to be polite to her. Why am I the only one who finds her annoying?! 'Go, Tanya!' says Fee as Tanya steps up to take her last turn. 'Win it for the team!'

I seize my opportunity for another go at interrogation. 'Did you and Tanya know each other before camp?' I ask as Tanya notches an arrow.

'Nope,' Fee says cheerfully, dashing my theory of them being close friends. 'She's a sweetie, isn't she? Always coming and asking if she can do anything to help.'

'Oh, really?' I deliberately keep my tone neutral. I watch Fee's face closely, looking for any signs that she's uncomfortable talking about Tanya – but I can't spot anything. Either she's a very good actor, or there's nothing to hide.

'Yes – she groomed Axel for me the other evening, which was very sweet of her. I gave her a team point for it.'

'Three points,' I say.

'No, only one. Oh, great shot, Tanya!'

The competition is over, but I can't focus on anything Nina says because my brain has stuttered to a halt. Fee only gave Tanya one point? But Tanya said Fee had given her *three*. And there were definitely three more stickers on the chart the next morning.

Did Tanya add more stickers to the chart when no one was looking? Or is Fee a top-level fibber?

*

As we sit down to dinner, Geraldine announces the team points for the day. Our blue team is in the lead again with twenty-eight points, but the red team is right behind on twenty-seven. 'SSG for the win!' exclaims Jessie, doing an air punch.

'I have to tell you something,' I say in a low voice, and quickly I tell them what Fee said earlier about giving Tanya one point instead of three.

But instead of outrage, my friends all look at each other before Daniel says, 'Ellie, I know mysteries are your thing, and all that. But it just sounds like there's been a mix-up. I mean, maybe Tanya misheard. Or Fee forgot that she'd given Tanya three instead of one. It's not a *crime*.'

'But it means the red team have got two more points than they deserve!' I object. Why isn't anyone else annoyed about this? 'It's cheating.'

'Ooh, Ellie.' Daniel sits back, his hands out in a defensive gesture. 'I don't think you should go around throwing out accusations like that. Especially without evidence. Remember when you all thought I'd stolen Luna from Starlight?'

'This is different,' I say stubbornly. 'There's something going on, and Tanya's at the heart of it, I just know it.'

'Ellie,' says Summer cautiously, 'do you think maybe you're taking this a bit far?'

I turn to Jessie. 'You get it, don't you, Jessie? Come on.'

But Jessie too is looking uncomfortable. 'Look, I know Tanya isn't exactly the easiest person to get on with . . .'

I lean back. 'I can't believe it! Fine – you know what? Fine. Don't believe me then.'

Molly says hesitantly, 'Ellie, it's not that we don't believe you –'

'Oh Molly, as if you care! You're in the red team – you're the one who's going to win if there's cheating going on!'

Abruptly, Molly gets up and runs out of the room.

There is an awkward pause, and the rest of the gang looks at me. 'Well, *that* was an overreaction,' I comment. Underneath, I feel hot and guilty.

'Um, Ellie, I think you were a bit mean,' says Jessie.

'What's up with Molly, anyway?' I say, shame making me sound harsh. 'She's like a little mouse sometimes.'

'She told me she was worried about her mum,' Summer says quietly. 'I don't know, maybe she's ill or something? Molly said she wasn't sure her mum would be all right without her at home.'

I'm a bit hurt that Molly didn't tell me that herself. We're meant to be friends, aren't we? 'Well, she didn't need to run off like that. I wasn't trying to be horrible to her.'

'No, but you can be a bit . . . forceful,' says Daniel. 'Sometimes you get a bit carried away.'

'It's just that you get really set on something,' adds Jessie. 'And then it's like you focus on that and don't see . . . anything else.'

'Wow,' I say, not trusting myself to say anything else. '*Wow*.' How many times have I asked Molly if she wants to talk to me? Loads! Have I been a good friend? Yes! And now everyone's accusing me of being insensitive!

I put my dinner tray on my lap and go over to the washing-up bay, where I tip the rest of my uneaten food into the bin and dunk my crockery in the soapy water, scrubbing it roughly with the sponge and piling it on the draining board. Then, without a backward glance and blinking away tears, I wheel out of the canteen and down the corridor to my room.

Once inside, I shut the door and burst into sobs.

Thurs 26th October

I didn't mean to upset Molly, but I just don't get her sometimes. If I have stuff I'm worried about, I tell my friends. That's what friends are FOR! And she seems super-sensitive to everything. Like when she found the games equipment, she was almost GLOWING, like it made her feel special, finding some stupid boxes! And when she doesn't get a team point in lessons, she looks REALLY sad, when it shouldn't be that big a deal!

And the whole discussion about the Mystery of Tanya and Fee and the Red Team Points – everyone just brushed it aside and started having a go at me instead!!!

I feel all rubbish inside. Like I am actually a bin on the inside, full of screwed-up wrappers and banana skins and single-use plastic that's choking the oceans. I feel like the rest of the group is still a group but somehow I'm on the outside.

I've never felt like that before with the SSG.

Maybe they don't want me in the gang any more.

I don't know what to do.

# Chapter 14

Mum comes in while I'm writing my diary, and I hastily stuff it under the duvet. 'How's it going, need a hand?' she asks brightly. Then she sees my face. 'Are you OK? Ellie, has something happened?'

'No,' I say firmly. 'No, I'm fine, I'm just tired.'

I don't want to talk to her about this. She'll be all sympathetic and that will make me cry again.

'It's been a busy day all right,' says Mum, her

gaze still concerned. 'I hear you did brilliantly in archery.'

'Yeah, it was fun.'

'Well, it's about toileting time. Shall we get you sorted so you can go back for karaoke?'

I swallow. I *love* karaoke. My karaoke song is 'Shake It Off' by Taylor Swift. I NAIL that song every time.

But I don't think I can face my friends again tonight. 'I don't want to,' I tell Mum, my voice tetchy. 'I've had enough.'

'Oh.' She seems surprised. 'Are you sure? You love karaoke.'

'Well, I don't tonight, OK?'

She frowns. 'All right, no need to talk to me like that.'

'I wasn't talking to you like anything.' You know when you feel all wobbly and horrible and it makes you be nasty to people?

'Watch your tone,' Mum warns predictably, her lipsticked lips thinning. 'And don't roll your eyes at me. I don't know why you're in such a mood.'

'I'm not.' (I am.)

'But even if you're not going back for karaoke, we still need to get you toileted.'

I stay mutinously silent while she helps me, only letting out an irritated huff every now and then.

'Look, Ellie,' she says eventually. 'I can see you're upset about something.'

She's right, but I'm so grumpy I can't acknowledge it. I just go, 'Huh.'

After another ten minutes, she finally loses her temper and says, 'If you can't behave better, I'm taking you home first thing in the morning.'

'What?! It's only Thursday. Camp doesn't finish till Saturday!'

'I'm not having you throw a toddler tantrum,' snaps Mum. 'You wanted to come to camp – we made it happen. If you've fallen out with your friends, that's on you to make it up. But if you continue to be rude to me, we're leaving after breakfast.' She fixes me with a glare. 'Understand?'

'Huhmm.'

'I beg your pardon?'

'Yes.'

She nods. 'Good. Now, I'm heading back to the lounge because I said I'd help Nina this evening. By the time I come back to put you to bed, I expect an apology.'

I bite my lip. 'I don't need you to put me to bed. I'm already on the bed.'

'Fine. I'll come back to make sure you've put yourself to sleep. Stay in your room and think about whether you want to go home tomorrow morning.'

The door closes behind her.

Well, that went well.

I reach for my phone and open the SSG group chat. But I don't know what to type. Instead, I scroll back through the pages and pages of messages: silly jokes, horse memes, photos, quizzes, bits of news from Starlight or Samira Kennedy, Jessie's idol and the celebrity who came to give out trophies at our summer competition. I can hardly believe so much has happened in such a short space of time. Meeting Summer, getting the gang together, Luna going missing, the Haversham Horse Trials, Jessie falling off Angus and getting concussion, the summer show with Samira . . . and now pony camp. There's no other group of people I'd rather hang out with. We just all . . . get each other. They get *me*.

Are they right? Am I too forceful?

Am I . . . insensitive?

I hate even thinking the question. Being insensitive is a bad thing. I care about my friends, don't I? I mean, I ask them how they are . . . sometimes.

If I am insensitive – and I'm not saying I *am* – how would I stop it?

I don't know how else to be. I'm just me.

There's a quiet knock at the door. 'Who is it?' I ask.

'It's Jessie. Can I come in?'

'I suppose.'

Jessie comes in, closing the door behind her. She looks awkward. 'I just wanted to see if you were OK.'

I shrug.

Hesitantly, she comes and sits on the end of the bed. 'Why haven't you come to karaoke? Are you sick?'

I shrug again. 'Just don't feel like it.'

There's a pause. Jessie twists her hands together and wriggles a bit. 'I thought you might be upset about what I said.' She pauses again, but I don't say anything. 'And then I thought about that time you helped me with something.'

I frown. 'With what?'

'Do you remember when I wanted to buy Summer a riding helmet because she didn't have enough money herself?'

'Yeah.'

'And Mum and I took her to the shop as a birthday surprise, and Summer got all upset and wouldn't talk to me?'

I nod.

'Well, you helped me to understand a bit about what she was feeling. And I thought . . .' She trails off, nervously. 'I thought maybe I could do the same thing . . . for you.'

I look at her suspiciously. 'Did Summer tell you to come and talk to me?'

Her face goes red straightaway. 'Er . . .'

I give a snort of laughter. 'Knew it.'

'Yes, but I wanted to anyway,' insists Jessie. 'I did! I just – you know I'm not good at this kind of thing.' She does a sort of smiley grimace. 'But I think maybe you and me are a bit alike. You know, when it comes to other people.'

'What do you mean?'

She pushes herself across so that her back is against the wall. 'I mean – we're the most confident ones of the group, right? Summer doesn't like being the centre of attention, and Daniel – well, he doesn't seem to care one way or the other. He just gets on with stuff. But you and me . . . we're leaders, we have ideas and make people listen to us. We like making decisions.'

I nod. I definitely identify with this. 'We get frustrated when people don't let us carry out our ideas.'

'Right!' Jessie exclaims. 'It's so annoying! Like we have these ideas and other people go: "Oh, I'm not sure . . ." and argh!'

I grin. Jessie can be quite funny.

'The others don't get it,' she goes on. 'When we have ideas and we make decisions, other people can get . . . I dunno, run over.'

I start to laugh. 'Run over?'

'Yeah, like we don't stop to think about whether everyone is on board – we just keep driving on, you know? I mean, when I decided to buy Summer a helmet, I didn't ask her about it. I just went ahead – and I really upset her.'

'So what are you saying?' I ask.

'Oh, I dunno.' She laughs. 'Summer gave me this big speech about listening and being empathetic and stuff, and I don't think I've done any of that. I think what I was *trying* to say is that if people don't agree with you, it doesn't mean they don't like you.' She pauses again for a moment. 'I don't get why you have to write Case Notes on every tiny thing, but it doesn't mean I think you're weird or an idiot or – or wrong, exactly. I still *like* you.'

'Oh,' I say in a small voice. 'I thought maybe you guys were fed up with me.'

Jessie bursts out laughing. 'Are you kidding? Who'd organize us if you weren't in the group? Who'd text in capitals if you weren't there?'

I throw a pillow at her. 'You make me sound like a pain.'

'Well, you are,' says Jessie, rolling her eyes. 'But so am I. And so is Summer, sometimes. And even your precious Daniel.'

'He's not my precious Daniel!' I protest.

'Whatever. Point is . . . um, I dunno. Just come back, yeah?'

I look down at my hands. 'What about Molly? Did I upset her?'

'Yes,' says Jessie bluntly. 'But only for a bit. She knows you didn't mean it.'

'I really do think there's something weird going on,' I say earnestly.

Jessie tilts her head to one side. 'Are you *sure*? I mean, don't get mad – but you're sure you're not taking a couple of coincidences and turning them into this big Mystery with a capital M?'

I'm about to argue back, but I take a moment to think. 'I get what you're saying. But I just *feel* that something's wrong. Honestly.'

Jessie looks at me for a long moment and then nods. 'OK. Well, like I say, I don't always agree with you. But if you *are* right, then it's not fair. And maybe we can find out one way or the other – without upsetting anyone.'

'Are you saying you'll help me look for proof?' I lean forward, my heart beating faster. 'Really?'

'Yes, but only if it doesn't mess up our last full day of pony camp,' says Jessie. 'I've actually been *riding*, Ellie – I'm having fewer panic attacks and everything. Summer even managed a canter today, did you see? We're all doing brilliantly and having loads of fun – I don't want to ruin it. Whatever we do, it has to be . . .'

'Subtle?' I suggest.

'I don't know what that means.'

'It's like – not very noticeable.'

'Oh, right. Then yes.' She smiles at me. 'We'll be subtle.'

I smile back at her. 'Thanks, Jessie.'

She holds out her arms. 'Summer would say we have to hug now.'

I laugh and she shuffles closer so we can hug. 'Tell Summer you did everything she said.'

**Ellie**
Hey, guys. I'm sorry for being a pain. And sorry I didn't make it to karaoke

**Summer**
Aww, we love you, Ellie. Jessie told us you were worn-out

**Ellie**

I am! And I can't believe I missed my chance to sing 'Shake It Off'! I hope someone did it for me

**Daniel**

Tanya sang it. She was really good

**Jessie**

DANIEL!!! Don't say that!!

**Daniel**

Well, she was

**Jessie**

Ellie can sing it better

**Daniel**

I've never heard Ellie sing

**Ellie**

Are you kidding, I AM AMAZING!! I AM BASICALLY TAYLOR SWIFT REBORN

191

**Summer**
Oh no, you made her hit all caps

**Daniel**
You can't be Taylor Swift reborn if she's still alive.

**Ellie**
ANYWAY you are all going to help me prove the red team is cheating, yes?

**Jessie**
No!! That's not what I said!!! I said we could maybe help find out if there IS something going on!

**Ellie**
Same thing 😊

**Daniel**
What do you want us to do?

**Ellie**
Does anyone know what the final points score was this evening?

**Jessie**
Not apart from the fact that the blue team is winning, yay!

**Summer**
I do. We're in the lead with 28. Then Red has 27, Yellow is on 23, and Purple and Green are both on 22

**Jessie**
!!! Summer, how do you remember all those numbers?!

**Daniel**
Wow, Summer!

**Summer**
I just like numbers. They're way easier than words

**Ellie**
Summer, you're a top detective

**Summer**
LOL. Can this detective get some sleep now? I'm so tired

**Daniel**
Me too. See you in the morning

**Jessie**
Night!

**Ellie**
Night!

Thurs 26<sup>th</sup> October

This has been a wild day. Mum came in just as I was signing off in the group, and I apologized and she said I could stay till Saturday as planned – PHEW. I know I was mean to her. I just couldn't seem to help it.

I was just starting to nod off when I thought I should message Molly to apologize. I said I was sorry I upset her, and that I hadn't meant to. The funny thing is, I'd be happy for Molly if she won something fair and square. She's really nice! I hope she is OK.

I feel like I've spent the evening apologizing!!! Saying sorry is EXHAUSTIFYING. I've done a quick update to my Case Notes. Tomorrow, I'm going to watch that points chart LIKE A HAWK. I want to know what every single point is for - and if someone's cheating (they definitely ARE) I will PROVE IT! AHAHAHAHA!

Zzzzzzzzz

Ongoing Case: The Mystery Cheater at Pony Camp

Location: Berry Farm

Date: Thursday 26th October

Time: 10.21 p.m.

Theory: Someone is cheating to make sure the red team wins the team trophy.

Suspects: Tanya, Fee

Suspicious events:

- Mud on Onyx
- Three missing kits from the yellow team
- Tanya getting three points for grooming Fee's horse when Fee said she only awarded one (which one of them is lying?)
- Bunch of flowers tied with red ribbon
- Missing games equipment found by Molly. (Who hid it?)

Evidence: practically none!

Plan of action:

- Continue to watch Tanya and Fee (involve the other SSG in this)
- Monitor the points chart closely
- GATHER EVIDENCE - only two days left!

**@starlightstablesyouth** Good morning, SSG fans!! Today is our last full day at pony camp at Berry Farm and we are RARING to go! In fact, some of the horses are so excited, they're REARING to go! See what I did there? This morning we're doing SHOWJUMPING!! I am so excited!! Then we have another Musical Ride rehearsal, and later there's another hack. Tomorrow we will be going home, boo! What are YOU up to today? Let me know in the comments!

#poniesaremylife #berryfarm
#ponycamp #ssg

# Chapter 15

It's a chilly morning with little spots of rain in the air. You can tell it's the end of the week because people are yawning at breakfast and definitely not bouncing with enthusiasm any more. Summer brings her plate to the table and then goes to fetch cutlery and comes back without it twice. 'I can't seem to think straight this morning,' she says, covering her mouth with her hand to stifle another yawn.

'*I'm* thinking straight,' I say firmly. 'Did anyone look at the sticker chart this morning?'

The others glance at each other. 'No,' says Daniel. 'Why?'

'There's another sticker in the red team's row,' I tell him.

His eyebrows shoot up. 'Really?'

'Really. Remember you said they had twenty-seven last night, Summer?'

She nods, frowning. 'Geraldine announced it at the end of karaoke, and I looked at the points chart before I went to bed.'

'There are twenty-eight in the red team's row this morning,' I tell her.

'No way. I'm going to look,' says Jessie. When she comes back, she's shaking her head. 'I can't believe it. They've got the same number as us now. But no one could have earned a point between bedtime last night and breakfast this morning – could they?'

'Hey, Tanya,' Daniel calls suddenly, spotting Tanya heading towards us with her tray. 'Did you get up early to groom Fee's pony again?'

Tanya stares at him in confusion. 'No, what are you talking about? Why are you asking?'

'Oh, no reason,' says Daniel, turning back to us.

Tanya rolls her eyes and walks past, muttering 'So weird' under her breath.

We all look at each other. 'How did an extra sticker get added to the chart?' I ask pointedly.

Molly says: 'It wasn't me,' and everyone immediately responds with cries of: 'No, of course not!', 'We know it's not you!', etc.

'I'm so sorry about what I said last night,' I tell her. 'I got carried away and I was mean.'

She smiles at me. 'Thanks, Ellie. I liked your message. My dad says I'm too sensitive. I need to toughen up.'

'No, it wasn't your fault,' I say. 'It was me.'

Daniel nods approvingly at me, and my face feels hot for some reason.

Jessie takes a breath. 'Ellie's right. Something is definitely going on. We need a plan.'

'I've got one.' I glance round and lean forward, and my friends lean in too. 'We need to stick like

201

glue to Tanya and Fee. They're our prime suspects. Tanya might not be blackmailing Fee, but maybe Fee is helping her for another reason – we can't cross her off the suspect list yet. Don't let either of them out of your sight.'

'It should be easy to keep an eye on Tanya since she's in our group,' says Daniel. 'But Fee might be more difficult.'

'I can help with that,' says Jessie. 'We've got a showjumping lesson this morning and I've already told Geraldine I don't want to do it. She said I should help out with chores, so I can follow Fee around the yard.'

'Brilliant!'

She grins. 'Who knew my anxiety would come in handy?' Summer squeezes her hand.

When we get to the stables, I give Elvis lots of kisses on his soft nose. 'We're going to *jump* today, Elvis!' I tell him. 'You and me, we're going to jump! How cool is that!' Something catches my eye and I turn to see Mum dash behind the stable block. She REALLY doesn't want me jumping. In fact, she tried to persuade me to sit this morning's lesson out. As if! I groom him and tack him up and have a quick skip out of his stable. He needs proper mucking out later. He's only been in there a couple of hours and the shavings are wet through!

Jessie gives me a thumbs-up as I take Elvis out of the yard. Poor Angus whinnies and kicks at his stable. He can see everyone else going out to have fun and he doesn't understand why he can't go too. But Jessie gives him a big hug and then heads over to Fee, saying loudly, 'What can I do to help?' I grin. Fee will have difficulty doing anything sneaky with Jessie by her side!

Rumana has set up some poles on the floor of the arena and two low jumps, a basic upright with a single pole, and a cross-pole, which is where you have two poles crossing over, making the middle part slightly lower than the ends. Mum comes to watch by the side of the arena, and I just know she's terrified, but I give her a cheery wave and a smile.

The first time Elvis jumps, he jumps MUCH

higher than he needs to, and I clutch at the reins in shock. Mum claps her hands to her mouth in terror. Anyone else would normally use their legs to help stabilize themselves, but I can't do that, so instead, I clench my stomach muscles and tighten my core, and I stay on, even though my heart is racing like a train. 'Well done,' says Rumana appreciatively. 'Elvis, were you showing off?'

Once I've taken a few deep breaths to calm my heart rate, I'm desperate to do it again. I did *not* expect to love jumping this much!

Daniel is flipping brilliant. I mean BRILLIANT. He stays focused and poised, and he looks like a professional. Rumana says: 'Are you sure you haven't done this before, Daniel?' in a shocked tone.

Daniel just shrugs and says, 'No, never.'

'Well, you're a natural,' says Rumana.

Daniel just sort of shuffles in an embarrassed way and I beam at him. 'You can do everything,' I say as we watch Kizzy go round.

'Oh no,' he says, sounding horrified. 'There's loads of stuff I can't do.'

'Like what?'

'Oh – you know. Stuff.'

I watch as he lines up Onyx for his next turn. I haven't yet come across anything Daniel can't do!

Summer and Molly are very nervous but they both manage to take their ponies over the jumps at a trot. Luna hops over like a rabbit and makes us laugh. Tanya's pony, Silver, refuses a LOT. 'Try to be steadier in the approach,' Rumana advises. 'Let him know it's not scary. You're tightening up, and that makes him think you're worried.'

'I'm not worried,' snaps Tanya. 'I've done loads of jumping.'

I bet she hasn't.

The lesson is over far too quickly for my liking. 'I think jumping might be my new favourite thing,' I say as we come out of the arena.

'No, thank you,' says Mum firmly, hearing this.

'Mum, remember that time when you managed to stop me doing that thing I wanted to do?'

She frowns. 'No.'

I grin at her. 'Me neither.'

Back at the yard we untack the ponies and give them a rub-down and some hay. I get into the stinky business of mucking out, and Mum comes to give me a hand, which is nice because manoeuvring around a wheelbarrow in a stall is awkward. When Mum is off emptying the wheelbarrow, Jessie sticks her head in. 'Hey.'

'Hey! How's the Fee-tracking going?'

'Brilliant.' Jessie laughs. 'She actually said to me at one point, "Jessie, why are you there every time I turn round?"'

I laugh. 'Subtle, were you?'

'*So* subtle. Anyway, she didn't get a chance to do anything unusual. But after lunch we've got another Musical Ride rehearsal, and I can't miss that. We'll have to hope she doesn't do anything then.'

'Right,' says Rumana. 'This is your last rehearsal before tomorrow's performance, so you need to work *together*.' She looks round at all of us with quite a hard stare. I glance sideways at Tanya, who happens to glance sideways at me at exactly the

207

same moment, and you could almost set light to something as our eyes meet.

Rumana goes off to the side of the arena to operate the music, and the rest of us gather in the middle. Jessie says, 'Shall we start by running through what we agreed on last session? Then we can stop and work out what needs to come next.'

'What did we agree on?' asks Finn. 'I can't remember.'

'Me neither,' says Luke.

I roll my eyes. 'Oh, this is going to go *brilliantly*.'

Once the boys have been reminded of the beginning of the routine, it actually goes quite smoothly until Summer suggests that one of us should be Elphaba, the green witch in *Wicked* who sings the song. Tanya immediately volunteers. 'I could hold a broom up while you all go round me in a circle,' she says.

'Why you?' I object.

'Why not me?' she retorts.

'It was Summer's idea,' I point out. 'She should do it.'

'I don't think it matters which of us is the one in the middle,' says Daniel in a reasonable tone.

'Exactly,' I tell him. 'So it should be Summer.'

'Oh, I'd rather not.' Summer squirms in the saddle. 'You know I don't like the spotlight.'

'I love the spotlight and the spotlight loves me,' declares Tanya with a laugh. 'I played Matilda in my drama club's production last term.'

I roll my eyes. 'Of course you did.'

'What's that supposed to mean?'

'Look, are we getting on with this or what?' asks Kizzy.

'*Fine*,' I say. 'Whatever.'

Of course, once Tanya gets to be Elphaba in the middle of the circle, she starts making her part even bigger. 'Elphaba has all these witchy powers. I could cast spells on the rest of you; make you go in different directions. You'd be, like, under my control.'

'That sounds cool,' says Daniel, and I stare at him in betrayed outrage.

'Is this the Tanya show now?' I mutter to Summer as we line up, ready to cross on the diagonals.

'Ellie, it's not that bad,' she murmurs back.

I bite my tongue as we practise crossing over diagonals (it's way harder than it looks). I just KNOW Tanya is basking in every single moment she gets to be the star. What's the betting she's angling for yet another team point too?

'Ellie!' says Jessie, as Elvis walks straight into the back of Angus. 'Watch where you're going!'

'Sorry.'

We continue to rehearse and Tanya continues to direct. Every single move is centred around her! She brandishes a broom handle with a few twigs tied to the bottom of it, and Silver doesn't like it at all, skipping sideways as it comes into her vision.

'You're spooking your own horse,' I tell Tanya.

She pulls up Silver sharply and glares at me. 'What is your *problem*, Ellie?'

'What are you talking about?'

'Are you jealous of me?' Tanya demands.

I let out a sarcastic laugh. '*Me*? Jealous of *you*? I think not!'

'You only have ten minutes left!' calls Rumana from the side of the arena.

We run through the whole thing twice more, and by the end, I'm feeling quite violent towards Tanya. I don't know why she gets under my skin so much; I'm normally really easy-going and get on with everyone. It annoys me even more that the others don't seem to mind her so much!

'You can decorate your ponies before the performance tomorrow,' Rumana tells us as we file out of the arena. 'We're supplying a load of chalks you can use, so have a think about what you might want to do.'

'Green manes!' exclaims Summer immediately. 'Oh, and I wonder if they have any green ribbon left like the ones given to the green team. We could plait green ribbons into the horses' tails!'

'That's a brilliant idea,' says Tanya, and I make a huffing noise. She snaps at me, 'Oh, shut *up*, Ellie.'

'Wow. *Rude*,' I say.

Back in the yard, the yard girls supervise the chores as usual. Elvis needs a drink, so I fetch a bucket and fill it with water. As it's filling up, I hear Tanya come past, and I accidentally on purpose flick the hose sideways.

There's a scream. 'What the—?'

I turn to see Tanya dripping with water. 'Oh, sorry, Tanya,' I say in satisfaction. 'Didn't see you there.'

'Oh, you are in *so* much trouble.' She gives me a venomous stare and stomps off.

I grin and say to Elvis, 'Don't care, it was worth it to wipe that smug look off her face.' He snorts at me as if he's agreeing.

The saddle has got quite mucky over the past couple of days, so I decide to give it a quick polish. I'm fetching the saddle soap and sponge from the storage room when I hear Fee talking to Hattie outside. 'Yeah, it's really close this year, isn't it? I think the red team might just edge it, though. Tanya's very competitive, isn't she? She keeps asking what their score is.'

I want to burst out, 'SHE'S CHEATING!' but I hold it in and head back to Elvis and the saddle, which I left hanging over his stable door.

It's not there any more.

I look around, puzzled. 'Anyone seen Elvis's saddle?'

Finn and Kizzy nearby shake their heads. 'Where did you leave it?' asks Kizzy.

'Right here, draped over the stable door. I was gone literally two minutes.'

Kizzy shrugs. 'Sorry, no idea. You could ask Tanya; she came past a minute ago.'

My mouth sets in a grim line. Of course she did. I know what's happened now. She's getting her own back for my water splashing. She's taken the saddle and hidden it somewhere.

Furious, I fling down the saddle soap and sponge and wheel myself round to the other side of the stable block, where Silver is looking over his door. There's no sign of Tanya. I turn around, wondering what to do. Where could she have hidden it?

Then I look back at Silver. 'Hey, Silver. Is there anything in your stable that shouldn't be there . . . ?'

You definitely shouldn't interfere with someone else's horse. But this is an emergency. And detectives have to take risks to find out the truth. With a furtive look round, I undo the bolt on Silver's stable door and encourage him out, tying him up to the ring outside. Then I slip into the open stable. A quick glance around shows me the saddle isn't here. Unless it's buried under the shavings? That would be a nasty thing to do: it could get properly damaged. I need a broom or a fork – something to poke at the shavings and see if there's anything hidden underneath.

A sudden scream from outside makes me jump. 'Where's my pony?' Tanya shrieks. 'Where's Silver?' She appears in the doorway, eyes wide with loathing. 'And what are *you* doing in there?'

'What do you mean, where's Silver?' I say defensively, wheeling towards her. 'He's right next to you, look . . .' I trail off.

The ring is empty. Silver has gone.

# Chapter 16

The world swirls and spins for a moment. 'He was right here,' I say faintly. 'I tied him up.'

Tanya goes into hysterics, screaming and crying, rushing from one end of the stable block to the other. 'Where is he?? I have to find him!' She rounds on me. 'This is all your fault! I can't *believe* you, Ellie!'

'Calm down,' I try. 'He won't have got far.'

This is true. Berry Farm is full of people and horses and someone will have spotted Silver by now and gone after him. But there's always the possibility that he manages to hurt himself, or someone else, in the meantime. He's a bit of a spicy pony. I swallow, a dark tangle of worry in my stomach.

People come rushing up. 'What's going on?' 'Why's Tanya crying?'

'Ellie let my pony out!' Tanya accuses, pointing at me viciously. 'She let him out on purpose! She's been mean to me since day one!'

'She didn't,' says Jessie fiercely. 'You *total* liar!'

'Ellie wouldn't do something like that,' says Summer.

But Daniel looks at me, and suddenly I want to burst into tears because it's like he *knows*, and I feel *awful*. 'I tied him up,' I say, my voice quivering. 'I did. Someone must have untied him.'

'Why are you trying to blame someone else?' rages Tanya. 'It's *literally* all your fault!'

'Right.' Fee takes immediate charge. 'You, you and you – head to the outdoor arena. You and

216

you – round the back towards the storage area. You, you . . .'

I cover my eyes with my hands. I don't want anyone looking at me. 'Oh, Ellie,' Daniel says sadly before running off to search with the others. Tears leak through my fingers.

It isn't long before Silver is found, though he takes a while to be caught because he gets completely freaked with everyone trying to approach him from different directions. By the time he's brought back

to his stable, Tanya hugging and kissing him and narrowly avoiding being trodden on, I'm hiding my face in Elvis's nose as he leans down over his stable door and nuzzles me.

I know Geraldine is going to come for me, and she does of course, flanked by Fee and Hattie. 'Ellie,' she says in a stern voice. 'I'm not a person who jumps to conclusions, and I realize I only have Tanya's side of the story. I'd like to hear yours.'

'I thought she'd stolen my saddle,' I say into Elvis's nose.

'Why would she steal your saddle?' Geraldine asks, astonished.

'Because she doesn't like me.'

'You splashed her with the hose,' Fee points out.

'I see,' says Geraldine. Out of the corner of my eye, I see Daniel approaching, and I wish he would go away. I don't want any of my friends to watch me being humiliated. But instead, he comes right past her and stands next to me, his hand on my shoulder. It's oddly comforting.

'So you thought she'd taken your saddle,' Geraldine continues, ignoring Daniel. 'Why didn't you go and ask her?'

'I did, but she wasn't there, and I thought maybe she'd hidden it in Silver's stable . . .' I grind to a halt.

'So you let Silver out of the stable so you could go in and look?' Fee sounds appalled.

'I tied him up!' I say defensively. 'I swear I did!'

'And did you find your saddle?' asks Geraldine, her voice icy.

I look down. 'No.'

'Where did you leave it?' asks Hattie.

I gesture to the stable door. 'On here.'

She steps forward, gently pushing Elvis's head to one side, and looks down over the door. 'Ellie, it's on the floor in here. He's standing on it.'

Oh no. I feel sick.

'Why didn't you just look over the door?' asks Fee.

I glare at her. 'From down here? Are you serious?'

Daniel opens the stable door and extracts the saddle from under Elvis's hooves. It looks decidedly the worse for wear.

Geraldine shakes her head. 'I'm gobsmacked, I really am. Twelve years of running pony camps and I've never had anything like this happen.'

I bite my lip.

She sighs. 'You'd better come up to the main building with me. I need to talk to you and your mum, seeing as she's here. Daniel, put that saddle in the tack room, please. Ellie, come with me.'

I daren't look up at Daniel as I follow Geraldine. We have to pass the end of the next stable block, where literally *everyone* else is gathered, and a sudden hush falls as I pass. I know everyone has turned to look at me, and I keep my gaze resolutely on the ground ahead. My face burns and my eyes sting. Now would be a really good time for the ground to disappear into one of those sinkholes you read about suddenly appearing.

The interview with Geraldine and my mum is deeply unpleasant. I feel like I'm in a police station under interrogation.

DCI Geraldine: Recording in session. Detective Chief Inspector Geraldine Pony Camp Organizer present, along with Suspect Ellie Horse Stealer and her mother. Please state your names for the record.

Ellie: Ellie. Not Guilty.

Mum: Shocked Mother.

DCI Geraldine: Thank you. Now, Ellie, on the afternoon in question, you were seen to be arguing fiercely with Innocent Tanya during a Musical Ride rehearsal — is this correct?

Ellie: She wanted to be the witch in the middle and the boss.

DCI Geraldine: But *you* wanted to be the boss, eh?

Ellie: No, I —

DCI Geraldine: I put it to you that you did. And then later you deliberately hosed her down in front of everyone.

Ellie: I may have accidentally splashed her.

Mum: Ellie! I'm so sorry, Inspector, I don't know what's got into her. I'm shocked. Shocked, I tell you.

DCI Geraldine: Did you or did you not let her pony, Silver, out of his stable?

Ellie: I did, ma'am.

DCI Geraldine: Were you or were you not engaged in a campaign of revenge against Innocent Tanya?

Ellie: She's not innocent! She's been cheating all week!

DCI Geraldine: These are very serious charges; do you have any proof?

Ellie: Not exactly, I —

DCI Geraldine: I thought so. This kind of behaviour is completely unacceptable, not to mention highly dangerous.

Mum: I'm shocked, as I may have said before. Shocked.

DCI Geraldine: Ellie, I'm going to offer you a deal. You may stay at pony camp until it ends tomorrow, but only on two conditions. The first is that you may not ride in the performance tomorrow morning when the parents arrive. You may participate in all other activities.

Ellie: What other activities? There's only a film and a barbecue tonight!

DCI Geraldine: Exactly. The second condition is that you apologize sincerely to Tanya.

Ellie: Grrr.

```
Mum: She'll do it, Inspector.

DCI Geraldine: She'd better. Otherwise
I'll  be  referring  this  case  to  the
Crown Prosecution Service. Interview
terminated.
```

All right, so it didn't go *exactly* like that. But nearly. And then Fee brought Tanya up to the office and I had to apologize to her in front of Mum and Geraldine and Fee, and it made me feel like A BIG PILE OF POO because although I *was* very sorry about accidentally setting Silver free, I was still convinced that the red team was getting illegal points. But who cares about a team point competition any more?

'I care,' says Daniel later at dinner. 'You were the biggest idiot ever, Ellie –'

'Thanks.'

'– but there's definitely something going on.'

I blow on my fingers. We're having a barbecue on the lawn outside the accommodation block, and the air is chilly. My hot dog is tasty though. I am with my friends and trying to ignore the hostile stares from other kids. Even though I've apologized to Tanya, it's clear everyone hates me for letting a pony go free. I'm not entirely sure I blame them. 'Don't let her go near your pony,' I hear one say to another. 'You can't trust her.'

It really stings. 'It's OK,' says Summer quietly. 'We're with you, Ellie.'

I give her a wobbly smile. 'Thanks, Summer.'

She smiles back. 'You made a mistake. We all do it.'

'I've made loads,' declares Jessie.

'Good evening, everyone!' calls Geraldine, standing up at the front. I try to hide behind Daniel. 'I'm sure you're all eager to hear the current state of the team points, especially as this is the last evening! Before I announce them, I should say that there is still a chance to win more team points tomorrow morning before the prize-giving, so the team in the lead tonight can still have the trophy snatched away before the end of camp!' She glances down at a piece of paper. 'So tonight, the yellow team is on twenty-nine. The green team is on thirty-one. The purple team is on thirty-four.' She pauses, and I hold my breath. Is the SSG team still in the lead? 'The red team is on thirty-five,' she continues. 'And . . . the blue team is two points ahead of them with thirty-seven points!'

My friends all smile happily at each other, but there are glares and mutterings from the other teams and I see Summer's face fall in response. Then Jessie notices and reaches to squeeze Summer's hand sympathetically. I feel AWFUL. Everyone else hates the blue team now because I'm in it. I've ruined everything for my friends.

Then I see Fee lean over to say something to Tanya, whose expression brightens, and my lips press together. They're planning more cheating! And I bet I know when. Tonight, when everyone has gone to bed – one of them will sneak out and add more stickers to the team chart.

There's only one way to prove my suspicions, and that's to catch them in the act.

I know exactly what I have to do.

Friday 27th October

I've seen loads of films with stake-outs. The detectives sit in their car outside someone's house and they eat fried chicken or doughnuts and drink coffee and bicker until something happens and then they rush out of the car, leaving it unlocked, and go fight the baddie.

This isn't a film and I don't have a car, so I'm having to improvise.

My Stake-out Plan

1. Sneak out of my room after lights out and go down the corridor to the canteen.

2. Conceal myself in the corridor just outside the canteen.

3. Start recording on my phone.

4. Wait. Possibly eat chocolate. (Crisps are too noisy.)

5. When Tanya or Fee turns up to put stickers on the chart, wait until they have actually done it and then confront them. Record the confrontation as evidence.

I don't know what I'll do after that. Part of me wants to go storming into Geraldine's room and shouting triumphantly that I've been vindicated (this is a good word. From the Latin meaning 'avenger', so it fits PERFECTLY). But I suppose the sensible thing to do would be to go back to bed and then tell Geraldine in the morning.

Plus I don't actually know where her bedroom is.


Possible problems with My Stake-out Plan

1. 'Sneaking out' of anywhere in a wheelchair is VERY DIFFICULT. Mum will make sure I'm in bed in my pyjamas. I will have to wait till she's gone back to her room and maybe ten more minutes before I get myself out of bed and back into my chair.

2. What if there isn't anywhere to hide in the corridor? It's a good thing my pyjamas are navy blue – at least they're decent camouflage.

3. Does my phone have enough charge? Charge it NOW!

4. What if I have to wait till like 3 a.m.???

5. What if T or F gets VIOLENT???

# Chapter 17

Mum comes in just as I'm writing the last bit, so I hastily stuff my diary back under my pillow. She helps me with the usual stuff but she's very quiet and looks kind of sad. I feel a pang go through me. Mum and Dad both work hard to make sure I can still do all the things I want to do despite my disability. She had to make sacrifices to come on the pony camp week with me, and now I've made a right mess of everything.

Impulsively, I put my hand on her arm while she's smoothing the duvet over me. 'Thanks, Mum. I'm sorry I was an idiot.'

She gives a little, tired smile. 'I know. Thanks, sweetie. I just wish . . . that sometimes you'd think before you act.' Then she kisses me on the head, says goodnight, and leaves.

*Ouch.*

I hear the door to Mum's room close, and I wait in the dark for fifteen minutes, watching the time tick by on my phone. Mum takes exactly seven minutes in the bathroom at home, and then she gets into bed and usually goes to sleep quite quickly. I daren't leave any sooner – I need her to be really sleepy so that she doesn't hear me moving about. I'm keeping my fingers crossed that our cheat is waiting for the building to be quiet too!

When the time's up, I reach across to my chair, transferring my weight into it. It sounds harder than it is – when you've been doing it as long as I have,

230

you get to know the knack. I unlock the brakes and wheel myself silently to the door, my phone in my lap.

The corridor is silent and shadowy, lit only by a night-light plug low down on a wall. Distantly, I can hear boards creaking as people upstairs move around. My wheels make no sound on the carpet as I edge carefully down the corridor. If I'm caught now, I have no reasonable excuse.

I take a moment to listen when I reach the turn in the corridor that will lead me past the front door and along to the canteen. I close my eyes so I can hear better – have you ever noticed that if you shut off one sense, the others are amplified? But apart from the faint upstairs creaking and a distant door banging, there's nothing from the nearby vicinity, so I move slowly round the corner and past the front door.

Up ahead are the double doors to the canteen, and on the wall to my left is the team points chart, the shiny round stickers catching the dim light. I count them carefully – they still have the same numbers as earlier this evening. Good – I've beaten the cheat to it! I look around to see where I can hide. There's a table, and a flip chart, and a tall case with glass doors on it. But no handy nook for my chair and me. Bother!

I push through the double doors to the canteen. Maybe I could hide on this side? But the doors close without a gap and the only windows they have are at so-called 'head height', which is fine if you're someone whose head is at standing-up height, but no use if your head is level with most people's waists. I'd have no idea if anyone was on the other side.

I feel my frustration rising. Tanya or Fee could be on their way right now, and I've got no way of spying on them! Maybe if I prop one of the doors open very slightly? I start looking for a doorstop or something I can wedge underneath a door – not that I can actually reach the floor without getting out of my chair . . .

'Argh,' I mutter to myself, and then I get THE FRIGHT OF MY LIFE as the double doors suddenly swing open, nearly bashing my knees.

Daniel, Summer and Jessie are standing in the doorway, grinning at me. 'All right?' says Daniel.

'*No!*' I hiss. 'You literally gave me a HEART ATTACK! I could have DIED.'

My friends let the doors swing shut behind them with a slight whooshing noise. 'We were sneaking down to bring you a midnight feast!' says Jessie, looking injured. 'We saw your room was empty and we came looking in case you were in trouble.'

'Shhh! Keep your voice down!' I say. 'They could be here at any minute!'

'Who?' asks Summer.

Daniels's eyes widen. 'Ellie ... are you on a *stake-out*?'

'Um ...'

'Without *us*?'

All three of them look at me in hurt outrage.

'Look, I haven't got time to explain,' I whisper. 'Fee or Tanya could turn up any minute to add illegal stickers to the chart.'

'But we're on the wrong side of the door,' Summer whispers, pointing out the obvious.

'I *know* that,' I say, annoyed. 'I was just trying to work out how to spy on them without being seen.'

Daniel pulls out his phone. 'I know.' He swipes the screen and taps it.

In my lap, my phone buzzes. 'What are you doing? Accept video call from you? What good will that do? You're right here!'

Daniel holds his phone up to the window of the door, grinning, and I suddenly realize.

'Oh! Oh my gosh, you're a genius!' Accepting the call, I can see what Daniel's phone camera sees – straight out into the dim corridor! 'It's not very clear.'

He rolls his eyes. 'You're welcome.'

Summer pulls out three packets of sweets. 'We can have our midnight feast while we wait.'

I smile. 'I love you guys.'

'We love you too,' says Daniel, and it's a good thing no one can see my face clearly in the gloom.

'How long do you think we'll have to wait?' asks Jessie, settling down on the floor next to me and accepting a cola bottle from Summer.

'I don't know,' I murmur. 'Surely not long. Fee would be missed from the yard girls' horsebox if she was gone too long, and Tanya's sharing a room, so –'

'Shh!' says Daniel suddenly, and I nearly choke on my strawberry lace. 'Someone's coming!'

Jessie, Summer and I stare at the screen of my phone. Someone is definitely moving towards us in the dark.

'I'm scared,' Summer whispers.

My heart is beating SO hard, and my breath is coming in little shallow gasps. The figure looks too big to be Tanya. It stops opposite the points chart and fumbles with something. Then, very clearly, an arm reaches out to the chart on the wall. 'This is it!' I say. 'I can't believe it! It's Fee – after all that! She must be a *very* good liar.' I end the call, swipe on my phone torch, and reach for my wheel rims. 'Open the door, Daniel.'

Daniel reaches for the handle, and then pauses and says, 'Wait, Ellie. I don't think it's –'

'Open the door!' I yell suddenly, and he yanks on the handle in shock, pulling it open. I swing myself

into the gap, holding up my phone torch. 'Trying to cheat again, Fee? Well, this time we ALL saw you!'

The figure throws up their hands in defence, covering their face. White hands. Not Black hands.

My jaw drops. 'What – you're not Fee? What the –'

A pale face bordered with red hair peeps out from behind the splayed fingers.

I gasp. My torch wobbles as my brain desperately tries to reconfigure itself.

'*Hattie?!*'

# Chapter 18

'Wh-what are you all doing here?' stammers Hattie. Her red hair is tousled and she's wearing a baggy jumper and wellies over pyjamas.

'*You?*' says Daniel in astonishment, which is exactly what I would say except my mouth has briefly stopped working. '*You're* the one who's been cheating?'

'But . . .' says Summer.

I finally remember how to think and speak. 'You've got a lot of explaining to do,' I say sternly, steadying my phone torch.

Hattie blinks and grimaces. 'Could you not point that thing right in my eyes, please?'

I lower it slightly. 'Don't think of running away. We've all seen you.'

'I don't understand,' says Summer. 'Why would *you* be cheating? Are you trying to help Tanya to win too?'

Hattie frowns in confusion. 'Help Tanya? No! I was trying to help *Molly*. She – she's not with you, is she? I don't want her to know any of this.'

Enlightenment dawns. 'You're Molly's cousin,' I say slowly. 'What's going on?'

Hattie sighs. 'Look, I don't know how much Molly has told you, but things aren't great at home. Her dad . . . he's a bit . . . well, he has some anger issues. Molly asked him if she could come to pony camp and he basically yelled at her about not emptying the dishwasher.'

'What?' I'm baffled.

'Yeah – he's just – he overreacts a bit. Molly's mum had to book pony camp and sneak her out of the house without him knowing. I heard he got angry when he found out she'd gone.'

'Is that why Molly's worried about her mum?' I ask.

Hattie nods. 'Look, I'm not sure I should be telling you any of this, it's private business. But I know you're Molly's friends.'

'We are,' I say firmly. 'We definitely, definitely are.'

Hattie gives me a bit of a smile. 'She's not very confident in herself. She's got very low self-esteem. I think her dad sometimes tells her she's no good.'

'That's horrible,' says Jessie quietly.

'So when she manages to do something, or win something – she just lights up, you know? I've seen her happier this week than in ages. And I just wanted to – to help her feel happy more often.' Hattie bites her lip. 'It started by accident – you know in your first lesson, Daniel and Jessie, you both got points? Molly was so disappointed she didn't have a point; she told me she didn't think she was good enough to be here, and maybe she should just go home . . .'

My friends and I look at each other.

'I tripped over in the yard,' Hattie continues. 'I stuck my hand in a patch of mud, and I was on my way to wash it off when I came past Onyx.' She looks at Daniel sheepishly. 'You weren't there; I think you'd gone to get something. Anyway, I – well, I knew the yard girls would be coming round to give points for well-groomed ponies, and I ... I wiped my hand on Onyx, so you couldn't get a second point, Daniel. I'm so sorry. I felt guilty as soon as I'd done it, but by then it was too late to wipe it off.' She looks at the floor.

'What about the flowers? And the yellow team's cleaning kits? And the games equipment?' I ask.

'The flowers were from Molly,' says Hattie. 'I swear they were! Geraldine agreed to fit Molly in at the last minute – I know she can be a bit strict, but she's soft as anything underneath. We didn't know if Molly would actually be able to come until the morning of camp. Geraldine was really kind about it, so Molly asked me to get some flowers that she could leave on Geraldine's desk as a nice thank you. I think she was going to write a note but then felt embarrassed, so left them anonymously.'

'And the red ribbon?' I ask.

Hattie shrugs. 'Complete coincidence. It wasn't Tanya's, I know that. I saw Molly's face when Tanya tried to claim the flowers were from her and she was completely shocked. She ran out of the canteen and I found her crying in the toilets.'

There's a sober pause. 'I didn't know that,' says Summer.

'Why didn't we notice that Molly was upset?' says Jessie, shaking her head.

'Because I was too busy trying to solve the mystery,' I say bitterly.

'Did you hide the mounted games equipment too?' asks Daniel.

Hattie nods. 'I thought if I could engineer it so that Molly was the one who found it, she'd feel proud of herself because everyone would be pleased.'

'But Fee was the one who told them to go and look there,' I say, frowning.

'No. Fee told her to go and look in the feed room. I said there was already someone looking there.'

'And there wasn't?'

'Of course not. I needed Molly to go look in the storage area. Fee nearly ruined it by sending Tanya along with Molly, but luckily Molly still found the stuff.'

'So you set up moments where Molly could win points – or at least, you stopped other people from winning them,' I tell Hattie.

She nods. 'The yellow team were pulling ahead

early on, so I hid their cleaning kits. I put them back later, I swear.'

'And you've *also* been sneaking up here at night to add more points to the chart,' I continue.

'Only the last couple of nights,' says Hattie defensively. 'You four were just too good at winning team points! I only wanted to make sure the red team could win in the end. No one else thought to count the points in the morning – no one else noticed they were different from the night before.'

Everyone looks at me.

'What?' I say.

'You and your eye for a mystery,' says Daniel, but he's smiling at me.

'Whatever,' I say, and have to clear my throat. 'The point is, what are we going to do about this?'

Hattie looks frightened. 'Please don't tell Molly! She'd be humiliated! She doesn't know about any of this – and I shouldn't have told you about what's been going on at home; she doesn't want anyone to know. *Please* don't tell her anything!'

I let out a long breath. 'I don't think we have to

tell Molly,' I say slowly. 'But, Hattie, if the red team wins tomorrow, it'll be because you cheated.'

'Does it matter?' asks Summer in a small voice. We all look at her and she shrinks at the attention. 'I'm just saying . . . if it makes Molly happy – does it matter? We don't *need* to win, do we?'

There's a pause, and Jessie says, 'No. We don't need to win.'

I'm astonished. Jessie is the most competitive of all of us!

'I agree,' says Daniel. 'We know we're a good team. We don't need a trophy to prove it.' He looks at me. 'Don't you think, Ellie?'

Everyone looks at me, and I don't know what to say. I understand what they're saying – I really do. In a way, I agree with them. It doesn't matter to *us* if the blue team doesn't win. Except . . . except the other teams have all lost points too. That's not fair. It's not about us. It's about fairness. Since I had my accident, I'm more aware than ever of when things aren't fair. If *we* decide we don't mind about the cheating, that's one thing. We can make decisions

245

for ourselves. But it's not fair for us to decide for everyone else too.

The pause lengthens and my friends start to exchange awkward glances.

'I . . .' I say, finding it hard to get the words out, 'I just think . . .'

'No,' says Hattie suddenly. 'You don't have to say anything, Ellie. I can't ask you all to lie for me. I'll go and tell Geraldine first thing in the morning, and she can decide what to do.'

I let out a breath. 'I'll come with you.' Hattie's about to object, but I plough on. 'I got the wrong idea from the start. I thought Tanya and Fee were the ones doing all this. I got obsessed with them just because I didn't like Tanya, and I took it too far. I get it now. I still think she's a pain in the bum, but she wasn't cheating and none of this is her fault.' I take a breath. 'I need to go and fess up. Tomorrow morning, just before breakfast, OK? You and me, we'll go and talk to Geraldine.' My stomach clenches at the thought. Geraldine is already cross with me. I hope this doesn't make her even crosser.

Hattie, with a sad nod, disappears off into the night back down to the stables, and the four of us head back up the corridor to my room. 'Don't wake my mum!' I hiss as we approach her door, but as we pass it, we can hear deep snores emanating from the other side, and we have to stifle giggles.

At my door, Jessie bends down to hug me. 'Nice work, Ellie,' she whispers.

I hug her back. 'Thanks.'

Summer bends down for a hug, and then Daniel says, 'Oh, see, now *I* have to hug too or I'll be the odd one out,' and he puts his arms around me for a moment and my stomach does a somersault.

'Right, yeah, thanks,' I babble, backing into my room and not looking at anyone. 'See you in the morning.'

They wave at me and vanish into the gloom of the corridor, and I close the door and stay very still for just a moment because the evening has been Quite A Lot. Shocks and questions – and – and hugs, and I think I'd better get some sleep now because tomorrow morning is going to be Quite A Lot More.

**@starlightstablesyouth** Hi SSG fans!! Here are the four of us on our very LAST morning at pony camp, boooo! We've had the BEST week ever, loads of new friends and their gorgeous ponies. We've done show jumping, cross country, archery, quizzes, games . . . and of course lots and lots of MUCKING OUT! This morning we've got our Musical Ride performance and we can't wait to show the parents our routine to 'Defying Gravity'! Then there's an awards ceremony and then we go HOME! Roll on the next pony camp, PLEASE!

**#ponycamp #ponylife #ponygames #musicalride #lastday #iloveponies #ssg**

# Chapter 19

You shouldn't believe everything you read online. I hit 'post' on my phone and see the happy photo of the four of us that I took *yesterday* morning, beside the words that leave so much out. The whole paragraph makes me sound excited and happy – and I'm not. I'm gutted not to be performing with the others this morning. What a sad way to end my first pony camp.

Mum comes in to help me get up and comments on how tired I look. 'Didn't you sleep?' she says.

'Mum,' I say, 'am I a nightmare?'

She gives a little laugh and then looks at me more closely. 'Why?'

'Just tell me. Am I a horrible person?'

Her expression changes. 'Oh *no* – no, Ellie, why would you think that?'

'You know how Nan says you can get hold of the wrong end of the stick?'

'Yes.'

'What do you think is the wrong end of the stick? I mean, does it have thorns or something?'

'Ellie, what's all this about?'

I sigh. 'I got it wrong, Mum. Tanya wasn't cheating. Fee wasn't cheating. It was – someone else. But I missed all the clues because I was looking in the wrong direction.'

She gives me a sympathetic look. 'I don't know what you're talking about, but it sounds pretty normal. Most of us get things wrong some of the time. We have an idea in our heads, and anything we see that doesn't fit that idea, we ignore. It's like putting blinkers on a horse.'

'What?'

She laughs. 'When you put blinkers on a horse, it can't get distracted. Let's say you wanted Elvis to focus only on what's right in front of him.' She puts her hands either side of her head, palms flat, like blinkers. 'Even if he turns his head, like this, he can only see a small portion of what's around him. Maybe you had blinkers on. You were only focusing on one person, so you didn't notice all the other clues.'

'Oh no,' I say, horrified. 'I am a *terrible* detective.'

She laughs. 'You're just learning – like we all are.'

I pick gloomily at a thread on my breeches. 'I have to go and see Geraldine this morning.'

'Again? Are you sure that's a good idea after yesterday? I don't want you to get into *more* trouble.'

'I have to explain,' I say with a shrug.

She gives me a hug. 'Well, I hope it goes OK.'


Hattie meets me outside the canteen, dark shadows under her eyes. We both avoid looking at the team-points sticker chart. Summer, Jessie and Daniel have gone in to breakfast, giving me supportive thumbs-up gestures. We've all had to pack up our rooms this morning and I don't know which makes me feel wobblier: leaving pony camp or facing Geraldine again. 'Ready?' says Hattie.

I nod.

Geraldine is in her office, a little room I've never been in before. Hattie plunges into her story first, and Geraldine's face turns serious. 'I know I did some stupid things,' says Hattie, her voice wobbling. 'I was trying to help Molly be happy.' She stops, swallowing.

I take the opportunity to dive in. 'And I got carried away . . .' I explain about noticing the things that Hattie had done but blaming Tanya and Fee. I hold out my Case Notes book.

Geraldine takes it with a look of bemusement. 'What's this?' She flicks through the pages. 'Is this . . . a detective notebook?' The corners of her mouth twitch.

'I read a lot of mystery stories,' I say defensively. 'I like being observant.'

Geraldine stifles a noise that might be a snort of laughter.

'The thing is,' I say, 'I spotted all the things Hattie had done but I blamed the wrong people. And that's why I did something stupid too.'

'I see,' says Geraldine, laying down my Case Notes book on her desk. There is a long pause – so long that I start to wonder if I should say something else – but then Geraldine sighs and shakes her head, and my heart sinks. 'Hattie, this is quite serious. I can't have a yard girl going around deliberately sabotaging things – I need you to be completely trustworthy.'

Hattie starts to cry. 'I'm so sorry.'

'I understand your reasons, but you've wasted people's time and caused upset. It's not setting a good example, which is what we ask of the yard girls. You're supposed to be role models. I'm often asked to write references for the people who work for me, and how can I write you a positive one after this?'

Hattie nods miserably.

'And, Ellie, I'm disappointed. Pony camp is about mucking in with everyone, pulling your weight, teamwork and social skills. Instead, you've basically been spying on people. That's what this is . . .' She waves my Case Notes book at me. 'Instead of bringing me any concerns, you went off on your own and caused a lot of trouble.' There's a pause, and her voice softens a little. 'But I can also appreciate that coming here this morning took a lot of courage from both of you. If you hadn't owned up, Hattie, I'd have been none the wiser – you could have got away with it, in other words.

'And, Ellie, it's always better to make a clean breast of things.' She glances out of the window. 'The sun is shining, and we have a lot to do today. Ellie, I reverse yesterday's decision. You may ride in the Musical Ride performance. Hattie, I expect you to behave impeccably for the rest of the morning – I can't afford to be a person down today. When the dust has settled on this, you and I will have a sit-down and talk about your behaviour and your future. Do you both understand?'

A wild excitement sweeps through me. 'I can ride?'

'You can.' Geraldine fixes me with a look. 'But no more cases today, Ellie. I mean it. You're here to ride and enjoy – just concentrate on that.'

I nod and take the book from her. 'Thank you. Thanks so much.'

In the canteen, my friends are waiting with a bacon roll for me. 'How did it go?'

I wheel myself to the end of the table. 'She said I can ride this morning.'

The Starlight Stables Gang erupts into cheers.

Molly, sitting with us, looks baffled. 'What's going on?'

I glance round and Daniel shakes his head slightly – that means they haven't told Molly about what happened last night, which is what we agreed. 'Oh, I went to apologize again to Geraldine,' I say. 'And she took pity on me.'

Molly's face splits into a smile. 'Oh, Ellie, I'm so pleased! That's awesome!'

As Molly and Jessie chatter about the Musical Ride, Summer leans over to me and whispers,

'What's Geraldine going to do about the team-points trophy?'

'I don't know,' I whisper back. 'She didn't say. I guess we'll find out later . . .'

When we get to the stables, Fee has the green chalks ready for us to decorate our ponies. 'Thanks, Fee,' I say gratefully, feeling extra guilty for suspecting her.

'No problem,' she says. 'The green ribbon has gone missing, though – I'll go and have another hunt for it.'

Automatically, I reach for my Case Notes book before remembering that I've left it with my bags. Then I remember what Geraldine said about enjoying the moment, and I scold myself: *Forget the mysteries for one day, Ellie!*

Molly ties Echo up next to Elvis so that we can decorate our ponies together. 'Last morning, Elvis,' I tell him, rubbing the chalks into his mane. It won't show up on the black part at all, but the white part of his mane is starting to look brilliant. Molly helps me do the bit by his withers because I can't reach up that far. 'Thanks, Molly.' I hesitate, watching her stroke the chalk down the long hairs. 'I think maybe I haven't been much of a friend this week.'

She glances back, startled. 'What do you mean?'

'I got carried away with my own imagination,' I admit. 'And I'm so sorry you couldn't be in our blue team.'

She thinks for a moment before saying, 'You know, it's OK. Mum says it's good for me to do things that I find a bit scary, like working with people I don't know. She says it'll help build up my confidence. It hasn't been as bad as I expected.'

I smile at her. 'That's good. Has it worked? The confidence-building thing?'

'I dunno. Maybe?' Molly turns back to Elvis's mane. 'Some things just make me panic. Like when people get angry with each other. Or when there's lots of shouting – even if people are having a good time and they're shouting in a happy way.'

I nod. 'Summer doesn't like it when things are really loud and frantic either. I think I'm one of those loud people!'

'Things can be a bit loud at home . . .' says Molly, still looking at Elvis's mane. 'It's nice to get away for a bit.'

'Are you worried about going home?' I ask, wondering if this is too personal a question.

She doesn't answer to start with, and I think maybe I shouldn't have asked – and then she says, 'I am a bit, yeah. I get told off a lot – I never seem to get anything right. And my mum tries to help but then she gets shouted at too.'

'By your dad?'

'Yeah.' I wait for her to go on, but she doesn't. Instead, she finishes up Elvis's mane and turns round to say, 'Ta-dah! What do you think?'

'Fantastic!'

I get that she doesn't want to say anything else and that's OK. I'll make sure I'm properly listening next time she wants to talk more.

'The parents are arriving!' An excited ripple runs through the stables just as Fee turns up brandishing a large roll of bright green ribbon.

Of course, my mum has been here all week, but

most of the kids here haven't seen their parents for five days. Geraldine stalks the stables, checking that everyone is behaving and that the ponies are in tip-top condition. They're not, to be fair. Elvis is pretty tired today, and Luna almost nods off while Summer is grooming her!

But at last it's time, and Rumana's group is going out for the Musical Ride first. Tobi lifts me into the saddle and says, 'This is the last time I'll do this – aww.'

The ten of us parade into the arena to claps and cheers from the parents and siblings. All the ponies are wearing green hair chalks and have ribbon woven into their tails – some more neatly than others! We take up our starting positions and as we wait for the music to start, I see my mum standing with Summer's dad and Jessie's mum and I smile and wave at them. I feel a little pang that no one is here for Daniel. His mum is so busy, and I'm guessing his aunt didn't feel able to bring all five of his brothers and sisters.

As the opening bars to 'Defying Gravity' start, I

touch Elvis lightly with the whips and he moves off with everyone else.

I'm never going to be Tanya's biggest fan, but I have to admit she really plays up her part. She's painted her face green with the chalks (which I don't think you're supposed to do, but she looks amazing) and has tied loads more twigs to her broom handle so it looks properly like a witch's broom. She does all the facial expressions too, casting spells on the rest of us.

The ponies don't do exactly what we want – at one point Onyx decides he doesn't want to go in the direction Daniel is turning him, and instead tries to skip round Echo, who turns to snap at him. Molly wobbles in the saddle but manages to get Echo under control, which earns her a round of applause from two women watching from the side. One has the same red hair as Molly and I'm guessing she must be Molly's mum.

I'm quite relieved when the piece is over. There were several moments when I couldn't remember what was supposed to happen next, so I had to look round to see what everyone else was doing. But everyone is cheering, so it didn't matter that we weren't perfect!

We dismount outside the arena and tie up the ponies and dash back to watch the other group do their *High School Musical* routine. 'Wow,' says Daniel. 'This is *really* good.'

'I'm going to beat my anxiety,' Jessie says determinedly as we watch the riders perform a complicated crossover movement in canter. 'Next year, I'm going to be in the advanced group.'

We have to untack and give the ponies a good rub-down before the awards ceremony. The grown-ups go off to have coffee (Jessie rolls her eyes and says, 'Coffee, YUCK!') and we do our last round of stable chores. I'm delivering a bale of shavings to my stable when I come to Silver's stable. Tanya is inside with a wheelbarrow and a fork. 'Hey, Tanya,' I call, before my courage can desert me.

She comes to the door, smudges of green still around her nose and hairline. 'Oh, it's you. What do you want?'

'I wanted to say I'm sorry again,' I say. 'Because when I said it before I was angry and I know you were too, and I've thought about it a lot. I blamed you for something that – that I'd imagined.'

She frowns. 'What?'

'It doesn't matter. I thought you were brilliant as Elphaba, by the way. You were right – it should have been you in the middle of the circle. Anyway, I just wanted to say that.'

I wheel off before she can respond. I feel a bit better for having said it.

'Hurry up, hurry up!' calls Fee, stalking down the stables and clapping her hands. 'Awards ceremony in ten minutes!'

Everyone hurries up. I feel a clutch of worry in my stomach. The awards ceremony – and the team trophy.

What has Geraldine decided to do about the team-points chart?

# Chapter 20

A table with a navy cloth has been set up outside the accommodation block. A bank of medals glitters in the light beside a single silver cup. The kids, reunited with their parents, sit excitedly on the huge tarpaulins spread on the ground. One of my wheels gets snarled up in the fabric and Mum struggles to free it. 'Can I help?' asks Molly's mum.

She and the woman she's with help my mum untangle the wheel.

'Thanks,' says Mum, smiling at them.

'I'm Molly's mum,' says Molly's mum.

My mum laughs. 'It's OK, you're allowed your own name. I'm Vanessa.'

'I'm Josie. This is my friend Robyn.'

'Shhh,' says someone because Geraldine has stood up and is looking expectant. Everyone quietens down. 'It's wonderful to see you all at the end of a fantastic week – and haven't we been lucky with the weather!'

She talks about what we've been doing throughout the week, and the progress everyone has made, and about a midnight feast that got out of hand that I knew *nothing* about – and then she moves on to the awards. There are medals for showjumping and cross-country; for bareback riding (Oscar's group), for the best rising trot, the best change of rein – even the best falling-off. Before long, half the kids are sporting medals and big smiles.

Jessie gets a medal for facing her fears. Summer gets one for finally achieving a canter. Daniel looks at me, and I know we're both wondering if either of us will get one.

'There's one person this week who has gone above and beyond,' says Geraldine. 'This person has volunteered for everything; has been endlessly – almost relentlessly – cheerful. They have offered to do extra chores, and they played a large role in the choreography of one of the musical rides you saw earlier. The Helper of the Week goes to Tanya!'

I clap along with everyone else. I suppose she *has* done all of those things, after all. Tanya goes up to collect her medal, beaming with pride. Jessie catches my eye and I give a kind of amused shrug.

'Every year,' Geraldine continues, 'the instructors nominate a rider as One To Watch. This means they think they've spotted genuine raw talent accompanied by a serious and determined attitude. *Everyone* here has the potential to become excellent riders – I want you all to remember that. Hard work and persistence can win out over anything. But this year, the instructors have nominated Daniel as someone they think could do great things in the future.'

Daniel's face is a picture of shock, which makes me want to laugh and cry all at once. I clap so hard my hands hurt. When he sits back down, he looks at me in disbelief and I just grin stupidly.

'This next medal is for Ellie,' says Geraldine abruptly, making me jump. 'Ellie has had a bit of a tricky week, but she has demonstrated great strength of character and we want to recognize that.'

Instead of waiting for me to wheel over to her, she comes to me and hands me the medal. 'Thanks,' I say, slightly embarrassed, especially as some of the kids are still annoyed with me about letting Silver out. Mum squeezes my shoulder as I tuck the medal into my lap. I'm not sure I want to put it on.

'Two awards to go,' says Geraldine, smiling round. 'And then it will be the end of another successful pony camp! This award goes to Most Improved Rider. This person came to us at the beginning of the week with very little riding experience. In fact, they didn't have a lot of confidence generally. But they have been a model student, doing all their chores without complaint, and have made very steady progress in their riding. This award goes to Molly.'

I see Molly's mum wipe away a tear as Molly goes up to get her medal, and at the very back of the group I see Hattie clapping so fast her hands are a blur.

'And finally,' says Geraldine, 'the moment everyone has been waiting for – the team-points trophy.' She pauses, as everyone's eyes turn to the gleaming cup on the table. 'I have to tell you that there has been a bit of a hiccup.'

I gulp, and clutch at the medal in my lap.

'Unfortunately when I took the chart down this morning,' Geraldine continues, 'I put it on a table in the canteen, where it accidentally got cleared away with the rubbish after breakfast.'

There's a sudden hush as everyone gasps and then waits to see what she'll say next. 'I do, of course, have a record of my own,' she says, and

there's a sigh of relief, 'and as everyone is well aware, instructors, the parent helpers and the yard girls were all able to award team points this morning too. The red and blue teams have led from the front all week, but at the very last minute, another team has slid up from third place to capture the top spot. Applause, please, for the purple team!'

My jaw drops, and I can tell most people are quite surprised – but the purple team members let out a shout of pure delight, and I swallow my disappointment that the SSG hasn't come out on top for once. Geraldine hands the trophy to one of the riders, and they take turns kissing it and passing it along, just like a football final. I've no idea what they did to win those points at the last minute, but maybe it's good that it wasn't either the red or the blue teams.

'And that's it!' says Geraldine, spreading her hands to indicate the empty table. 'Thank you all for coming and for making this week so enjoyable. Have a safe journey home and we hope to see you all again next year!'

'Can't I stay here forever?' Molly begs her mum as everyone starts to get up.

Her mum smiles at her. 'Sorry, love. We have to go home.'

Molly's face falls. 'I know.'

'But,' her mum says, glancing at her friend Robyn, 'we're not going *home* home. Not today. We – um – we're going to stay with Robyn for a bit.'

Molly looks confused. 'What about Dad?'

'He's – he's very busy with work,' says her mum. 'I thought it might be better if we give him a bit of space.'

I watch Molly's face and see a dawning relief, and I feel a kind of burning ache in my chest for her. My parents drive me mad, but at least my home is a safe place to be. 'See you at school,' I say, impulsively reaching for a hug.

She squeezes me back. 'Thanks, Ellie.'

'School?!' says Jessie in disgust. 'Oh no, I forgot all about it!'

Everyone laughs.

'We didn't win the trophy,' I say quietly to Daniel as people disperse back to the stables to load the ponies.

He looks at me with those pale blue eyes. 'Do you mind a lot?'

'No – no, not really. But I think it was my fault we didn't win.'

He smiles. 'Nah. You're not *that* important, Ellie.'

'Hey!'

He dodges, laughing, as I try to aim a punch at him. 'I'm not kidding! Alex and Olivia from the purple team got up early this morning and went round the entire accommodation block tidying away any rubbish and resetting the lounge furniture and everything. Nina gave them an extra five team points.'

'*Five?!*' I stare at him, my mouth open. 'Five points? On the last morning? *Five?!* But that's basically cheating!'

'They got up at six o'clock,' Daniel says with a shrug.

'I can't believe it!' I say. 'They totally did it just to get points on the last morning.'

'Well, it worked. And I heard Alex say he couldn't believe how messy everything had got in the lounge because it had been tidy last night. He reckoned some of the kids must have sneaked down to have a midnight party in there. *No*, Ellie.' His hand shoots out to stop my arm as I reach behind me. 'This is not a mystery for your Case Notes!'

I roll my eyes. 'I wasn't going to! I've got something for you, hang on.' He releases my arm and I dig into the bag on the back of my chair. 'There were some things left over in the snack area this morning, and –' I hold out a chocolate mini roll – 'I thought you might like to replace the magical mini roll with another one.'

His eyes crinkle at the corners as he smiles. 'How do you know this one is magic? It didn't come from that magic disappearing shop, did it?'

'No,' I admit. 'But I whispered a spell to it. So it's magic now.'

'What kind of spell?'

'I can't tell you that,' I say, feeling reckless. 'You'll have to find out if it works.'

He laughs and pockets the mini roll. 'Never change, Ellie.'

Saturday 4th November

Going back to school was kind of disappointing after pony camp. They still haven't sorted out what to do with me during PE. BUT Miss Mathyruban has been replaced with someone called Mrs Doyle and she is SO nice. She has a daughter who has cerebral palsy and who uses a wheelchair, so she knows LOADS about wheelchairs and disability. She's drawn a detailed accessibility map of the school and figured out all the short cuts and the danger areas, and she's going to share it with all the staff too. School will never be as fun as pony camp, but I think it might have fewer Annoying Things now that I've got Mrs Doyle to help.

Today, all four of us were at Starlight Stables for the first time since pony camp, and it was SO GOOOOD to be back!! Jodie and Sooz were having an argument about paint colours for the new stable block, and a kids' party came in just as the rain TIPPED down and there was CHAOS because it was too wet to go riding, and these little kids went absolutely BONKERS, some of them crying and others getting cross. Poor Sooz was in DESPAIR.

And then Daniel offered to teach them to juggle, and I showed them how to do wheelies in my chair, and Summer said she could draw anything they wanted, and Jessie said she could run a hobby-horse showjumping competition . . . and all of a sudden they were all having the BEST TIME as the rain drummed on the roof and everything got very, very silly and LOUD and Summer had to duck out for a bit because the noise got to her.

And when the kids all finally went home, the mum of the birthday boy said she'd never had such a successful party before and could she book us again for next year?!

Jessie's mum went out to a nearby shop and bought cake and the four of us sat outside the office on plastic chairs as it stopped raining. Daniel got cream on his nose and didn't realize, and Summer, Jessie and I couldn't stop giggling. Then Molly texted me to say she was having the best time at her mum's friend's house and that they were going to stay there at least a month. I showed the others and we all agreed that Molly deserved lots of nice things and that maybe we should bring her along to Starlight at some point.

Jodie and Sooz said as we were all so brilliant (NATURALLY) we could take the ponies out for a woodland walk. Dad rolled his eyes and said we were meant to be going home, but I begged and begged so hard that in the end he said we could stay.

Jessie's mum and my dad walked behind the four of us but quite a long way back, so it felt like it was just the Starlight Stables Gang: me on Elvis, Daniel on Onyx, Summer on Luna and Jessie on Angus. Just us walking through the soggy woods, with mizzle in the air still and puddles on the ground. And it was AMAZING.

Nothing will ever beat the feeling of being out on horseback with my friends. Even the feeling of solving a mystery. And there are mysteries EVERYWHERE, aren't there? Loads of them, waiting to be solved.

But Geraldine is right too: sometimes it's important just to enjoy what you're doing right now and not look for complications. So that's what I did today. Lived in the moment and enjoyed every minute.

Case closed.

# Acknowledgements

Thank you for reading what is now Book 3 in the *Starlight Stables Gang* series. It's been such a great experience going on this journey with Summer, Ellie, Jessie and Daniel. I'd like to thank my co-author Jo for helping me turn a jumble of ideas and experiences into a series about growing up, inclusivity and ponies. Jo has been a constant support and great friend along the way.

The Riding for the Disabled Association is an incredible charity that enriches the lives of over 17,000 disabled children and adults through their 500 RDA Centres across the UK. I've been a supporter of this amazing charity for a number of years and have been able to see first-hand the incredible work they do to enrich people's lives.

Ellie's character is in part inspired by some of the incredible people I have met at RDA events over the years. The RDA are hoping to expand the number of people they work with to 35,000 over the next few years, but this is only made possible by charitable donations. If you are at all able to, they would love any support you can give.

Natasha Baker OBE is a multiple-gold-winning Paralympian who has been an invaluable help, providing insight into growing up and riding with a disability.

Team Tutsham is a charity riding school that supports disadvantaged and vulnerable children and young people. I'm really proud to say I am a charity patron for them, and a lot of the Starlight Stables is inspired by the amazing work that they do.

Thanks for reading!

**Esme**

*With additional thanks to:*

Carol Barraclough at the Spinal Injuries Association
(www.spinal.co.uk)
Brian Abrams, AKA 'Grandad Wheels'
(www.grandadwheels.com)
Alice Summersbee at Riding for the Disabled
Association, Abingdon (rda.org.uk)
Natasha Baker OBE (natasha-baker.com)
Lewis Hemingway and his mum, Diane
Joanna Sholem

# Have you read the first Starlight Stables Gang adventure?

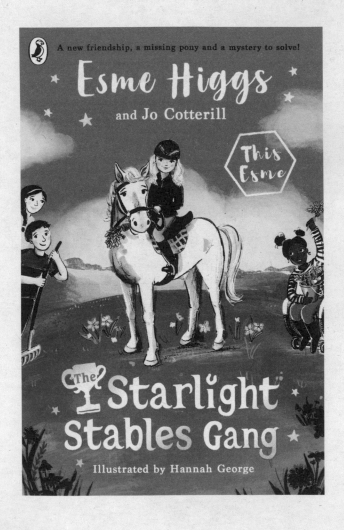

# Join the gang in their mission to save the stables!

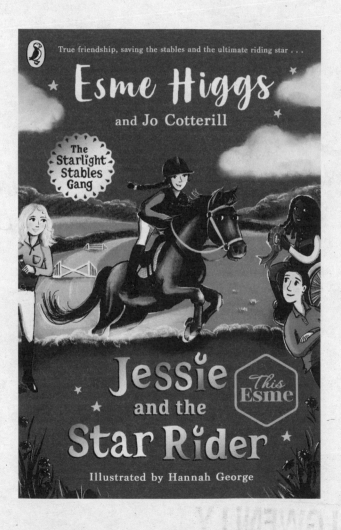

True friendship, saving the stables and the ultimate riding star . . .

## Esme Higgs
and Jo Cotterill

The Starlight Stables Gang

Jessie
and the
Star Rider

This Esme

Illustrated by Hannah George

PILLGWENLLY
Pill 13/02/24